THE KEY TO THIS WHOLE ENTIRE THING

SHORT STORIES

CHADD VANZANTEN

KNOWLEDGE FOREST
PRESS

Published by Knowledge Forest Press
P.O. Box 6331
Logan, UT 84341

ISBN-13: 978-1-949078-07-7
Jacket design by Knowledge Forest Press

For Amanda

Contents

JUST WAIT FOR THE ANSWER

This girl is so quiet. You may have misjudged just how quiet she really is. There are things you know about her, things you don't. She doesn't listen to jazz or classical music. She's not sure what she wants to major in. She rides horses. Ambivalent about seafood, probably doesn't like it, probably ordered it because you did, and you ordered it to impress her, but you don't think it worked. She is a runner, ran track in high school, ran the 1500 and the mile. Eyes blue like a backcountry lake. She sings, loves musicals, and was in all of her school plays.

This is all just trivia, though.

There is only one thing you know about her for certain—that she is awfully quiet—but there's not a lot you can do about that anymore. Your time is just about up.

The waiter brings the check. You help the girl put on her coat and together you go out into the night and the rain in the parking lot.

"Tonight was great," you tell her.

She nods and grins. That's all she does.

The asphalt shines in the darkness like a great spill of ink. You walk her to the car and open the door and she gets in. Rush around to the other side and you get in.

Streetlamps glimmer wet and bleary through the windows. For a few seconds, you don't look over. She's there in the passenger seat and you figure maybe she'll say something if you can keep yourself from looking over.

But she doesn't, and so you do, and when your eyes meet, she turns away. Not in a way that suggests she doesn't want to look at you, but more like it had taken her by surprise. There's no more than eight inches separating the two of you, no sound but the rain. It makes a noise like radio static.

To fill up the quiet, your turn on the car, and when that doesn't help, you begin to talk at her, and you keep talking for a while. About dinner, about school, and finally, desperately, about the weather.

"Sure got cold in a hurry," you observe. "It was gorgeous this afternoon."

She peers up through the window at the wet black sky as if to confirm this.

"My stupid car," you continue, "the windows fog up so bad. I'm sorry." You wipe the windshield with your palm, with your sleeve, and then you switch on the defroster. "I have to run the defrost and the AC at the same time when it's like this."

"Mm."

"Yeah, the evaporator fins in the AC unit condense the moisture out of the air, like a dehumidifier. It's a trick I learned. See, it's already starting to work. There's really not much difference between a dehumidifier and an air conditioner."

You're not sure if that is entirely true.

2

But she laughs, and hearing it makes you laugh, and that feels like progress of a sort. Then you both sit quietly again in the watery light of the car in the parking lot as the defroster breathes a rough and continuous sigh.

A raindrop creeps down from the top edge of the windshield, joining with nearby droplets until it becomes a rivulet that courses down the glass and out of sight like a tear. This girl has said nothing since the two of you got into the car and she appears quite content to keep doing so. You gnaw at the inside of your cheek to stop yourself lecturing further on the physics of automobile climate control.

Maybe a laugh or a glance from this girl holds more meaning than that of another. So, you recalibrate, adjust your expectations. Because there's something you plan to say to her. Something heavy.

You love the girl.

She probably knows, but it's time you said it to her. You rehearsed it earlier, in your bedroom, to your reflection in a mirror, so that it would come out right. It didn't go very well. It felt dishonest to try to manufacture a moment like that between two people, to force it into the open that way. You thought maybe it should happen more naturally. "Organically," as you've heard some people say. But you want it to happen, and you want it to happen right, and so you have prepared your remarks, and you're gauging the mood. And certainly it's important to you for her to furnish an answer, so you're trying to find the right moment to begin, like a pilot reading the wind and searching for someplace to land. You scan her landscape.

In the meantime, you say, "You know, I was surprised. I never thought you'd be into a sappy movie like that one. You know, that kind of sappy movie."

She shifts in her seat. Or maybe that was a shrug or some cryptic utterance of body language that you failed to catch.

"No," she says, nodding, "I like movies like that. Sappy ones. Corny. It was good." She looks over as if to turn the matter back to you.

"Right," you say, "it wasn't too bad. The movie, I mean. It was okay. For that kind of movie."

"Yeah. For that kind of movie, it was a good movie."

You stay quiet for another minute or two, silently offering her every opportunity to expound.

She doesn't accept.

"Well, so," you breathe, "tomorrow."

She only nods. But when you look at her this time, she doesn't turn away. You remove your hat (as you rehearsed), switch off the defroster, and turn in your seat to face her.

You speak her name. Then you tell her, "I love you. I do. And I've been wanting to say it."

Then you nod. Once. As if to punctuate it. To let her know that you're through speaking for the time being. Or maybe forever, for that matter. At this point it's hard to say. The effect that she is having on you could very well drive you to such extremes. You ponder monasteries, vows of silence.

Because it didn't come out exactly the way you rehearsed. Not hardly at all. There was something you wanted to say beforehand, to transition into it. There was more to it, and there was a certain cadence you wanted to affect. But the moment has been created now, and it begins to unfold around you. And it unfolds around the girl. She played a role in it, too, is still playing a role with her reticence. And so you learn that any such important moment must be forced into existence, or else it couldn't exist at all. Like a line of words in a love letter, or a parting embrace—they are deliberate acts. They never just happen.

The girl puts her face in her hand and cries a little. This was definitely not part of your rehearsal, nor was it featured in any of the instances you pictured. But you know what's going on. She cries because she leaves tomorrow. She has a scholarship at Northwestern, four states east. You're moving further west, to Oregon. In the morning, she'll be gone. A week after that, you will wade into the Pacific Ocean for the first time, and you will likely never be together with her again. You haven't decided what this means or what can be done about it. So, you take her in your arms and hold her, and you keep holding her for a while. She squeezes you hard, buries her face in your shirt. You breathe in the smell of her and pull her softness against you. Through her sobs she says your name in a plosive whisper, and you feel it on your neck.

If you lose her, it will be a year before you move beyond it, and the pain will last much longer. Some of it might never go away. And so you learn something else in the dim light of that inky parking lot. Love is a girl sobbing on your neck, and the price of love is loneliness.

When the girl settles back into the passenger seat, your shoulder is damp. She sniffs, wipes her face with her fingertips, and says nothing. All is quiet but the rain. It streaks the windows. Your cheeks grow hot and you watch the girl for signs.

She sits still, arms folded across her middle. Her back is straight, head tilted forward. On her face is an expression that is neither smile nor frown. You cannot see her blue eyes beneath her long eyelashes. If there is any signal in her stillness, you lack the ability to read it.

Then she looks up. Her arms unfold and her hands come to rest in her lap, one soft petal cradled in the other. Her gaze meets yours and her lips part. She draws a breath, and if you thought what you had to say to her was heavy, just you wait for the answer.

ALL THE WESTERN STATES

Deanne's family originally came from one of the big, rectangular states out west. Colorado or Montana. I could never remember which one because the one I thought was Colorado is actually Wyoming and the one I thought was Wyoming is really Montana. But it didn't matter because Deanne was born in Idaho and she eventually moved to Washington or Oregon—whichever one isn't on the top. So, in a way she was from all the western states. She was western. She looked western, acted western, sounded western.

That's what first attracted me—she was miles of open space.

I told her once, "Your eyes are blue like the sky you always see in pictures of Yellowstone."

That got her. I was mostly just trying to sound romantic, you know—poetic or lyrical. Her eyes were blue and beautiful, but apparently the Yellowstone Line worked better than I'd planned. She had to swallow and press one hand between her breasts to process that one.

But then another time I told her the cookies she'd just baked tasted like damp cardboard from a pizza box, which I thought was way more witty and definitely more expressive than the admittedly obsequious Yellowstone Line, but it was also the first time I ever made Deanne angry with me. She didn't get angry easily, so this is relevant. It was the part about the pizza box that tipped the scales, I think. That was the detail that I thought really brought the line to life, the detail that drove the point home. Apparently Deanne thought pizza boxes were constructed of some lower species of cardboard, and bringing their kind into an argument was hitting below the waist.

We'd been together for almost six months when I came up with the Pizza Box Line. Most of the other girls I'd dated had gotten angry with me several times before we even went out. Not Deanne. It took uncommon effort to make her angry. This made me suspicious, of course. I worried that it was a sign of emotional problems, or some complicated plan to make me look foolish. I was disappointed to learn it was neither of those.

She said, "Why get angry? Anger makes you bitter."

I said, "Oh, I'm well aware of that."

We first met when Deanne moved into the apartment across from me. One day at the beginning of the semester, she said hi to me in the hallway. Naturally, I assumed she wanted to borrow something, or get directions to Harris Hall, but she actually just wanted to say hi. I told her I didn't know many people who said hi for the sake of it. If any acknowledgment seems called for when I encounter a stranger, I'm really more of a press-your-lips-together-and-nod kind of person. Saying "hi" or "good morning" was a custom I'd heard of, something society once accepted but now deemed a little dangerous, like putting candles on a Christmas tree.

"Where I'm from," she told me, "we say hi to be nice."

"Where I'm from," I told her, "if someone's nice it usually means they're getting ready to rob you."

"That's so sad," she said.

Not only did she mean it, she was right. It was sad, and that was something I hadn't really thought of until just then.

"You should come to the game with us later," she said, as though this might serve as consolation for my entire upbringing.

"I've never been to a football game," I said.

"Oh, then you've gotta come," she said, clutching my coat sleeve, shaking me. "We're gonna win!"

She was right about that, too. We won. The Wildcats always won with Deanne in the stands. I imagined the players on the field would somehow spot her in the matching hat, scarf, and mittens she'd knitted in the school colors. The players would point at her and she'd grin that western grin, her nose and cheeks flushed but her blue eyes sparkling under the stadium lights.

In the huddle the quarterback would say, "Did you see her? That country girl in section F?"

They'd all nod, breath smoking out from their face masks.

"We gotta win this thing, goddamit," he'd growl, "win it for her!" and he'd point at her again and the rest of them would roar savagely and raise their thick arms into the air and Deanne would wave and grin more brightly, as if that were possible.

She was just that elegant. Not evening-gown elegant, not elegant like a champagne glass, but elegant like a plowshare or a pronghorn antelope, like she'd been designed by the genius of maximum simplicity and efficiency. The short, straight hair, high cheekbones. So striking, so tall. Breasts compact but perfectly shaped. Genius. And her high, soft voice—like a combination of a water organ and the bells they play at Christmastime in certain churches.

It didn't matter what Deanne said, her voice always sounded like music. She could say, "I got really bad diarrhea from that salsa they serve in the cafeteria," or "Ew, there's a big wad of earwax on my headphone," and I'd want to wrap my arms around her and kiss her mouth to drink the sound of her.

And so those big animals on the football field would throw the ball or kick it or run it whatever the hell it took to win, and at some point I realized there will always be men to win games for Deanne and her type, not just to earn their love, but simply because they exist.

Unfortunately, that kind of raw and startling elegance comes at a price. Deanne couldn't be evening-gown elegant even if she'd wanted to be, just like a plowshare could never be a silver teaspoon, and a railroad spike could not be a hat pin. It'd be a put-on if she tried, just an actress reading lines.

For example, her favorite movie was "The Lion King." She didn't know who Truffaut was, or Brakhage or Imamura.

It was the same with food. She'd never heard of berbere or tapas or kimchi—she preferred Kraft macaroni and cheese.

"Don't laugh at me," she said, pouring out the electric-orange cheese powder. "Where I'm from, we just eat simple stuff like this, but we always eat together, as a family."

"Where I'm from, we eat with the people we like. We only eat with family when somebody dies."

"That is so sad," she said. Again, she meant it. Again, she was right.

That was Deanne's super power—she meant every single word she said. And when she had something important to tell you, she'd hug you first and then tell you. Or she'd tell you while she was hugging you.

And so when Deanne grabbed me and put her lips to my ear and whispered, "I'm falling in love with you, Charles," well, it was (as they say out West) big medicine.

She moved in with me. I watched "The Lion King" with her once, but she didn't seem to think I was clever when I asked her if the heavy christological subtext of the movie was overt or unintentional.

I ate the macaroni and cheese she cooked in my 200-dollar copper saucepan. She wrinkled her nose when I suggested trying the instructions with raw milk and truffle oil.

None of this bothered me very much at first. I assumed after I made her some really good seafood polenta, or after we'd watched "8 ½" or "Solyaris," she'd come around. I assumed that I could tame her, guide her down from the Rockies and into the city. But she told me flatly and repeatedly that she didn't like jazz or classical music or modern art museums or weird movies. She told me didn't like seafood. It wasn't that she didn't like scallops or the strong flavors of salmon—she didn't like seafood at all.

"It all just tastes so fishy and gross and makes you wonder where it came from. I do like fishsticks, though."

"Of course you do."

What I didn't understand is that the western states, the really big ones, are bigger and higher and farther than you think.

One night she said, "Another foreign movie?"

I came back with, "Sorry, they didn't have any episodes of 'Little House on the Prairie'."

But she was impervious to that sort of acid. "Oh, really?" she moaned. "Dang it. I love that show."

When I took her out for Latin-Thai food for the first time, she said, "You don't have to keep taking me to these places where I can't pronounce anything on the menu. I'm fine eating at home."

"Me, too," I said. "I'm just never sure what kind of wine pairs with a broccoli-and-cheese Hot Pocket."

"Oh, nobody drinks wine with Hot Pockets," she said. "Just beer would be fine."

When we went home that night, Deanne wanted to make out, so I played some Schoenberg on my phone and Deanne just about jumped out the window.

Oddly, it was the subject of butter that put the most miles between us. You can't cook without real butter, let alone bake. Everyone knows that. But Deanne rarely touched any real butter. She used that stuff in the plastic tub called "I Can't Believe It's Not Butter," which, by the way, really must be the most presumptuous product name ever conceived. A battalion of jesuit missionaries couldn't make me believe it was butter.

That's what ruined her cookies. The recipe called for butter, but she wouldn't use butter, and that margariney goo was too damn oily. It was like an artist's conception of butter, by a not particularly talented artist, an artist who has only heard stories of butter.

Deanne's mother Gayle evidently used butter

substitutes the whole time Deanne was growing up, though whether this was a cost-saving measure or a dietary concern I never found out. She came out from Idaho to visit Deanne once, but I never got up the courage to ask.

Either way, it wasn't entirely Deanne's fault that she preferred I Can't Believe It's Not Butter, which, by the way, really ought to come with some kind of abbreviation, if for no other purpose than to assist couples who are arguing about it. It's impossible to make a point when you have to say that whole name every time. I suggested we shorten it to "It's Not Butter" since that's the one part of the name which is actually true. I thought that was pretty clever. If Deanne did, she wouldn't say.

One thing that really was hard for me to believe was that a family from out West could lead a largely butterless existence. My understanding was that Idaho was basically one continuous field of potatoes, with little herds of cows kept here and there and old wooden dairy churns on the front porch of every farmhouse to make the butter when the potatoes were ready to bake. But apparently at some point the people of Idaho had gotten tired of all the milking and churning and had turned to hydrogenated substitutes made in food labs. Deanne said she'd never even heard of Irish butter or clotted cream or ghee. And I could understand learning to tolerate margarine, and maybe even becoming partial to margarine while growing up with it and eating it every day as a kid, but what I really couldn't believe was that Deanne kept on eating it after she grew up and moved out.

"Your mother's not here," I said on the Sunday afternoon of the Pizza Box Line, as she pulled her cookies from the oven. They were flat and stiff and oily. "How can you use that fake butter when there's actual grass-fed butter right next to it in the refrigerator?"

She shrugged and said, "Mine tastes more buttery."

"Deanne," I said. "Nothing can taste more like butter than butter."

"I never said it tastes more like butter," she said. "I said more buttery."

"Butter is, by definition, the most buttery thing there is."

But I could already see her next move, and she saw it, too. Deanne was rustic, but she wasn't stupid.

"That's not true," she said after a pause. "Sugar is more sugary than a sugar beet. Altoids are more minty than real mint. Right? They're curiously strong."

Of course she was right. But at that point I needed to know what it took to stop her, to make her understand how backward and primitive she was despite her open-range beauty and terrifying sincerity—if anything could do that. Besides, I'd never lost an argument to Deanne, and I wasn't about to let my first defeat be about margarine. As I considered how long it would take her to find a new place and move out all of her things, I opened fire.

"This cookie is like wet cardboard from a pizza box. It's vile. I can't believe you think this is a cookie."

That slowed her down. I won't say it stopped her in her tracks, but she definitely felt it. She folded her arms testily, but the hurt expression on her face made it clear she considered me the injured party in the matter.

We didn't break up that day, didn't break up until almost a year later, and it wasn't about butter or cookies or my futile attempts to show her out as a cultural hayseed. It wasn't even really my fault at all in the end.

14

Deanne graduated, for one thing, and she applied to grad school in Washington. Or Oregon. The one that's not on top. I heard she eventually married a hippie guy from out there. I used to see her online sometimes but I haven't in years.

Deanne unfolded her arms, crossed the kitchen, and took the cookie from my hand. She examined it, turning it over in her hand for a second or two, and threw it in the garbage can. Then she put her hands on my shoulders and came close.

She said, "Charles, where I'm from, we just don't say things like that to each other."

I considered this and replied, "Where I'm from, that wouldn't even be considered an actual insult."

She said, "That's just sad."

I said, "Yeah, you're right. But so am I."

Deanne nodded, gave me a hug. "Then I forgive you," she said.

She meant it, and that's what really hurt.

TOO SOON FOR GUNS

I don't know where Glen got the idea I would ever want to go pheasant hunting. Least of all after everything that had happened. It might have been because six years ago I once may have said, "Oh, I love pheasant hunting," but Glen never listened to a word I said back then, so if that's what it was, it's not really my fault.

And even if he had been listening, he had to know I said it because I was engaged to his daughter at the time. Deanne was crazy about me, but I had to work much harder to impress Glen and Gayle and the rest of her family, so for our whole engagement I was the biggest and most wretched suck-up they'd ever seen. I ate liver and onions to appease Gayle. I ate Rocky Mountain oysters on a dare by Deanne's brothers. If Glen had said, "Ray, let's you and me get undressed and cuddle awhile," I'd have unbuttoned my shirt and said, "Glen, that's just what I was thinking."

I didn't think I'd ever win him over completely. I was a little too different from his boys. I had long hair. Deanne and me didn't go to church and never had kids.

I drove a Honda. The brothers were all churchgoing farmboys who drove Chevy pick-ups and wore their hair short. They all had lots of kids and when they said they loved pheasant hunting, they meant it.

We also had no interest in sticking around Boise, Deanne and I. That seemed to bother Glen even more than my Honda. He didn't like his kids moving away, even though almost all of them did.

"I just don't see what's in Oregon that ain't here," Glen said to Deanne when she told him we weren't staying. "Boise State is right here. There's jobs right here."

"We just want to look around for the best opportunities before we settle down, Dad," said Deanne. "Don't worry, we'll come back and see ya, maybe come back for good."

I've spent a lot of time wondering where I stand with Glen and Gayle now that Deanne's gone. Do I belong to this family? They say I do, but they'd have to say that. And do they blame me for Deanne? The first time I saw Glen after the accident, I could see it on his face: "I told you to stay here. I told you not to move."

But the first thing Glen said to me was, "I do not want you blaming yourself for this."

I said, "I appreciate that, Glen," but I wasn't sure what I was thanking him for. "Thank you for not wanting me to blame myself for this, Glen." Is that what I meant? Is that what he meant? He was just trying to make me feel better—I was thanking him for that, I guess—but I feel like it's pretty dark that he would think I'd blame anyone except the person who hit us.

It was good of Glen to say. That's what I kept telling myself. But there is so much guilt and blame. So, I'd go over his exact words again. He said he didn't want me blaming myself, but should I anyway? Did he? If he really thought it wasn't my fault, that's what he should say, right? "It wasn't your fault." Which is not what he had said.

And there was a chain of evidence there. When I looked Glen in the eyes, I saw it. If Deane and I hadn't moved, we wouldn't need to travel for Thanksgiving. And if we hadn't been traveling, we wouldn't have been driving "that Honda" out on I-84 that night in the snow. And if we hadn't been on I-84 that night, that blue Nissan minivan that lost traction would have veered into someone else's lane, not ours. And so on.

Gayle went a lot easier on me than Glen. As soon as she showed up for the funeral, she appointed herself my manager and spokesperson. When I would shut down, she would step in. Like when I'd zone out and dwell on some stupid thing for thirty minutes, an hour, Gayle had my back. I thought a lot about the ambulance for some reason—how it was so grimy and old. Most ambulances are immaculate, brand new. Deanne's was in real bad shape. I'd sit thinking about what something like that means, and meanwhile one of Deanne's brothers would come over and tell me it was time to go somewhere or time to eat, but I'd just go right on thinking. That's when Gayle would materialize, pat my back and say, "I don't think Ray's hungry right now."

In fairness to Glen, I should say that he kept trying to absolve me, but I guess I just couldn't trust him. Maybe he'd caught on to the way I felt, because just as I was ready to go back to Oregon after the funeral, he told me I should come stay with them for a week. I told him I'd stay two, just to see if he'd try and back out. He didn't. In fact, out of nowhere, he started calling me "son." He'd never done that before, and I could tell he had a hard time getting used to it. He'd tack it on where it didn't fit, like maybe Gayle put him up to it.

"Now, when you use that downstairs toilet," he'd say, "you gotta jiggle the handle after you flush. Son."

After dinner the house would get really quiet. Glen and Gayle wouldn't say hardly anything. Even the presence of their dead daughter's husband in the house couldn't break up their quiet dishwashing collaboration, their regimented TV viewing schedule. They still watched the news on network television at night. I found that very nostalgic. I'd sit in the living room with them, almost more to watch them watching the news than to watch the news myself. It was just like watching TV with my folks in our living room when I was a kid—the images flickering in their eyeglasses in the darkened room, the sound of droning crickets at the window.

When the news was over, I'd go down into the basement and get in Deanne's old bed. Gayle had no compunction about bunking me there.

She took me down to the room on the first day of my visit, and we stood together in the doorway, looking in but not going in.

"Small," said Gayle. She flipped on the lightswitch by reaching around the door jamb and making an upward-sweeping motion with her arm. "But it's still a good bed. You can toss those stuffed animals on the floor. I'll put 'em back later."

A sodium arc lamp stayed on all night somewhere among Glen's outbuildings, casting a shaft of light through Deanne's little basement window like a stationary moonbeam. It lit up Deanne's small study desk and her ancient computer. Pearl Jam poster on the paneled wall. Taped to the mirror above her dresser were clippings from the local paper about her at the state track finals and her forays into musical theater long ago. I could just make out her newsprint face, and I looked at it each night as I tried to sleep.

Mornings were a little better. I'd get up late and Gayle would have breakfast ready, trying to keep things warm until I finally woke up. While I sat and ate, Glen and Gayle would talk about things we might do, like take a trip together, the three of us. Then I'd go back to bed. Glen didn't like that, so after a few days he made me come with him while he walked his dog Nixon around his sprawling property, which he called "the Place."

"If you felt up to it," Glen said one morning as we followed the dog past the potato cellars and pole barns, "you could help me do a brake job on that truck."

"Yeah," I yawned, pocketing my hands against the chill. "I could hand you the wrenches or something."

He talked about other things we could do around the Place but never did—a shed that needed painting, fruit trees that needed pruning. He suggested going up to Table Rock for a hike.

"Oh, I'd like that," I said.

But I know for a fact I never said I'd like to go pheasant hunting.

Technically, it's not even fair for me to say I "don't like it," because I have never been pheasant hunting and know almost nothing about it. I once answered "yes" when Deanne's brothers asked me, "want to go pheasant hunting?" and I spent time in their company while they shot up some pheasants. But that was years ago. And in the even more-distant past, when I was in scouts, I fired a shotgun to ready myself for a future pheasant-hunting event that never occurred.

But I have never posed an actual threat to any pheasant.

I surprised myself by objecting at first, by trying to beg off. Glen was not a person who people gladly or easily said no to. In fact, he'd never really even asked me if I wanted to go.

As I emerged from the basement and sat down for some of Gayle's pecan waffles, Glen asked me, "You up for all day?"

"Yeah," I said, blinking, taking a sort of quick personal weariness inventory, "I guess. Sure."

"Good," he said, nodding. He'd eaten his waffles already, and he was sipping coffee and looking at a newspaper. "After you finishing eating," he went on, "we'll go out and see if we can't shoot a couple birds. Son."

I looked up from my waffles, wondering if it was a good idea to go someplace remote with Glen while he had a gun on him.

"Birds?" I asked.

"Pheasants," said Glen. The way he answered so quickly made me understand he was hoping he wouldn't have to elaborate but kind of knew he would.

"Oh," I said, "pheasants. Right."

"No hurry," said Glen without shifting his eyes from the paper. "Whenever you finish up."

I took that to mean I had something like three minutes to finish eating. I looked around for Gayle, but she'd already started clearing the table and had gone into the kitchen. I poked my waffles and chewed my bottom lip.

"We'll drive out to a place I know," said Glen. "Take Nixy with us. See if we can shoot one or two. It'll be good for us." He turned the paper over and snapped it flat and taut.

"Ya know, Glen, I haven't been hunting in a while," I said. "Or even at all," I wanted to add. Where was Gayle?

Glen waved off my protest like it was an insect buzzing into his personal space.

Gayle came back.

"Me and Ray are gonna head out and shoot a couple birds," said Glen.

Gayle took her appointed station at my side and I tried to hide the sigh of relief I breathed. I waited for her to say, "Oh Glen, Ray doesn't want to do any silly hunting today."

But she didn't.

She instead patted me on the back and said, "Oh, that sounds nice," and unless I was still partially blind with grief, I'm pretty sure I saw her and Glen trade a secret little nod before she went back into the kitchen with another load.

The only other woman in the room was Mrs. Butterworth, so I stared at her awhile. She was no help. She stood next to my plate, hands clasped across her generous, translucent waist, wearing an expression I read as, "Will there be anything else?"

I went to Deanne's bedroom and looked through my bags for something warm enough to wear. All I had was a black hoodie. I put on two flannel shirts and the hoodie and then sat on the bed, listening to Glen thumping around in his study.

"Gayle, where did you put that green shoulder bag 'a mine?" he shouted. "Gayle? Did you move it? Where did you move it to?"

"You put all that stuff in the garage," Gayle called

back.

Glen cursed and I heard him clomp up the stairs and out the garage door.

Soon he clomped back down and knocked on the door of Deanne's bedroom. I opened it from where I sat on the bed. Glen stood in the doorway in this wool coat and cap. He looked around inside but didn't come in, as if some barrier were still in place there, one that I was audacious enough to cross but not him. I waited for him to say something, but then I realized that he was hoping he wouldn't have to say anything, and so I stood up to see what he would do. He turned and left and I followed him into the study.

Glen produced a key and opened a gun locker.

"Twenty gauge, twelve gauge." He touched each gun with his middle finger. "Four-ten, another twelve, and that one's a twenty-eight. These birds always flush long. Pick your poison."

I didn't know if I should put some thought into my decision, or if I'd even been given enough information to choose. There was a time when I knew what some of those numbers meant, but I couldn't ask for a refresher now. In a few more minutes the woodstove heat of the house would melt Glen in his coat and hat. He looked at his watch. Twelve gauge shotguns were the only kind I had any experience with at all, but I assumed picking that one was too easy, childish maybe. I considered the others but had already forgotten which was which.

Glen chose one of the twelve-gage guns, the pump-action kind. Then he pulled open a drawer in the bottom of the locker and sorted through the ammunition there.

"You know," I said. "Maybe I'll just tag along. I don't even have a current hunting license right now." This was true but disingenuous; I had never had a hunting license at any time.

"We can get you one at the filling station," Glen said. He picked up the other twelve gauge, a double-barreled Winchester, and handed it to me. "Here. Just take that one," he said.

I followed him outside to the truck. A mist hung over the Place. Our breath smoked in the cold.

A half-hour later we stopped for the hunting license and then I was zoning out in Glen's pick-up as we drove out through the pastures and ag fields. Nixon stood on the big tool chest in the truck bed. The mist had retreated and the autumn landscape glowed with a coppery tint. After a while Glen slowed and pulled the truck off the road.

I just knew he had something he wanted to say to me. It seemed like something Glen would do—devise some long drive so that he could put me off my guard and have it be just him and me alone and then pull over to tell me something he thought I really needed to know. Something like, "You sleep too much," or "You should quit smoking," or "You ought not to've moved away with her."

The emergency break made a ratchety noise as Glen pulled it.

He said, "This is it."

I waited for Glen to come out with it. Whatever *it* would be. But he stayed quiet, so I looked over at him and he looked back at me and we looked at each other across the space between us.

"This is what?" I asked.

"It," he said flatly, gesturing with his chin at the view from the windshield. "We're here."

I looked out on a series of cropped hay fields lying in

the sun like vast hemp doormats.

"Oh. Yeah," I said. "Yeah, this looks great."

We got out of the truck. Nixon hopped down from the bed and stuck his nose in the dirt. Glen got out and put a box of Remington shells on the fender.

"That enough for starters?" he asked. "You a good shot?"

"Oh, I'm probably a little rusty," I chuckled.

Glen inserted a handful of shells into his shotgun and worked the pump. He dropped a few shells into his coat pocket and then stood looking at me.

"Shells?" he asked, nodding at them.

"Right."

I took two shells from the box, but couldn't open the gun with them in my hand, so I put them on the truck. One of them rolled down the fender. I flinched to catch it but Glen snagged it first. He put it back in the box and then took hold of my shotgun barrel, which I had allowed to stray in his direction. I apologized and pointed the gun at the ground. Then I realized I didn't know how to load the gun at all, so I turned and tilted it blindly.

"This is a lot different than what I'm used to," I said.

The wooden stock was a beautifully stained and lacquered, and just over the trigger housing there was an oval of brass etched with a pheasant taking flight. You could tell it had some age to it, and quality.

"Wow, Glen, this is a really nice gun. You sure you want me messing with it?"

"Here," said Glen. He thumbed a lever situated in plain sight between the two barrels, and the gun fell open by the breach.

"Right, okay," I said. "For some reason I thought that was the safety."

Glen walked out into the morning, as if he'd withstood as much bumbling as he could on one hunting trip. He whistled up Nixon, and the dog ran ahead, snuffling down the edge of the field.

I inserted a shell in each barrel of the Winchester, closed the breach, and the gun boomed deafeningly, blasting my father-in-law square in the ass.

Glen spun about and took one halting step, as though he thought he might walk it off. Then he collapsed stiffly into the hay stubble.

I dropped the shotgun and ran to him. Nixon barked at me ferociously, lunging, teeth clacking. Glen's face was drawn into a terrible grimace, his lines and wrinkles tight and pale. I pulled off my hoodie, meaning to cover Glen or prop up his head, but I was babbling something even I couldn't hear over Nixon's barking.

"Nixy!" roared Glen. "Enough. Sit."

The dog instantly settled down. So did I. Nixon turned in a circle and sat, licking his chops in a pathetic, jittery way. I bundled up the hoodie and put it under Glen's head.

Glen's voice went to a sort of low buzz. "Ray," he said.

"Yeah Glen?"

"You shot me in the ass."

"I know I did. I am so sorry."

"Wasn't your fault," he said. "It was too soon for guns, maybe."

"Maybe. Yeah."

"Ray."

"Yeah Glen."

"Wasn't your fault," he said, and he looked me in the face.

"I appreciate that, Glen." Hey lay back onto my

bunched-up hoodie and somehow managed to look almost comfortable. I fumbled in my pocket and took out my phone to dial 911.

"Ray."

"Yeah. Glen."

"Think I'm gonna pass out."

"You're probably going into shock."

"Doesn't hardly surprise me. Been awhile since anybody shot me."

I looked at Glen's ass. There was quite a bit of blood. I heard the dispatcher pick up the call. Glen nodded at me and I nodded back. I told the dispatcher what had happened and she told me to hold on a sec so I turned back to Glen and said, "You're going to be fine."

"Yeah," said Glen. "I expect we both'll be."

X-ACTO

No one has to tell me how great Bridget is. After six months together, I know everything about her.

It was no accident that old boyfriends called her on a weekly basis. No accident that every time I ran into my old roommate Trent Gleason, he said, "Sooo, how're things with you and Bridget?"

Not: "Hey, James, how's your new place?" Never: "Hey, James, you been golfing lately?" Always: "Sooo, how's things with you and Bridget?"

The thing about me and Trent is that we hate each other's guts. I actually feel bad about that. People shouldn't hate. But he feels the same way about me, so maybe it's okay.

Because this goes back quite a while. Back to college. I think Trent stole some girl from me and he thinks I stole one from him. We probably didn't really have as much to do with it as the girlfriends did, but that's how we saw it and so now we hate each other. It's like a rule.

Of course, we can't admit this, can't show it. If I tell Trent I hate him, or if I let him know by the way I act, that means I'm threatened by him, and he wins. And vice versa.

We've been at it for years, this little dance. When we see each other around town, it's very friendly. We have to be nice to each other, which just makes everything worse because we really do honestly hate each other but we can't be honest with each other or ourselves.

That's why he could ask about Bridget—because he knew I'll be nice to him. He's trying to force me into saying it: "I hate your goddamn guts."

It's not that I worried about Trent stealing Bridget. She's embarrassingly loyal. One time we were at Spooky's playing pool and she slapped some guy for coming on to her. Slapped him right across the face, like a movie star. And she could be one, too—the hair, the smile. You're not going to find a prettier girl, not in this town.

I don't know how, but Trent must have heard that me and Bridget had problems. We did. It wasn't the usual, though. I liked her. She liked me, though I feel like I'd have put a stop to that sooner or later in any case. But she wasn't jealous or clingy or frigid. The problem was something totally different, something I never saw coming—she was always presenting me with some part of her body and asking me, in the nicest possible voice, "Will you pick this? Will you pop this? Will you peel this for me?"

Bridget loved having things peeled and plucked off of her body. It was like a Zen thing for her.

"It actually regulates my emotional energy level," she told me without one ounce of irony.

I spent one whole Sunday afternoon peeling her sunburn. Peeled every square inch of her back. One piece was the size of a dollar bill and it made a sound like duct tape coming off the roll.

She said, "Ooo, that was a good one."

Other couples go for walks in the park, bike rides, coffee. What am I doing this Sunday? "Oh, not much, just peeling my girlfriend."

She'd get out of the shower and I'd hear, "James, can you come in here for a sec?"

That's how it started. The day she moved in, she called me into the bathroom after a shower. She was twisted around, trying to see her shoulder blade in the mirror.

She said, "Babe, can you see this? Is it a zit or what?"

At first I pretended I couldn't see it.

She said, "Right here. Right where my finger is."

"There's nothing right where your finger is."

"Well, I can feel something. You must not be looking."

"You mean this?"

"Ow! Yeah, that. What is that?"

"I do not know."

"Well, does it look like it belongs there? Can you pick it off? Can you squeeze it?"

I said, "You want me to squeeze it?"

She said, "Yeah, go for it." Then she braced herself on the towel rack like we were in some western, and I was getting ready to take a bullet out of her.

I worked on it for five or six minutes. It finally popped. A bunch of pus came out, and blood. I think I was in love with her, but I wasn't ready for pus. Is that selfish? Is it selfish to say, "I love you but I don't want your pus on me"?

Things got worse. Lancing blisters, plucking wild kinky hairs from unexpected regions of her body. Everyone has little zits and blemishes, but most people are embarrassed about that kind of thing. Not Bridget.

She put me in charge of it. Anything she couldn't identify or remove on her own was my responsibility.

She'd say, "Hey, remember that big blackhead we found last night?"

I'd cringe. "Yeah?"

"Well, you didn't get it all the way out. Here."

That's when she'd whip out the Little Black Bag, a nylon zipper pouch with tweezers and gauze and stuff. Like a tool kit for the pseudo-medical maintenance of her body.

She said, "If those tweezers aren't gonna do the job, there's an X-Acto knife in there you can use."

One time she crashed her bike and got a big road rash on her calf. It turned into a million little scabs, like strawberry seeds. They snagged up her tights and socks, so every night she had me picking them off. You won't find a sexier pair of legs, not in this town, but I got blood and skin under my nails. That's not sexy.

And if you think she's got great legs, take a look at her feet one time. They're perfect. Her toes are straight and even, with little perfect toenails. I used to kiss the top of her foot on the blue lines of her veins where they traced up into her ankle. But then she introduced me to the foot smoother. It's like a plastic chicken egg with a little cheese grater on one side. You're supposed to rub it on the rough parts of your feet to smooth them out. The shavings collect inside, like a pencil sharpener, but instead of wood and graphite dust, it's all full of dead human skin in powder form.

She put me in charge of that, too. The first time I emptied it out, I tried to pull it apart instead of twisting it to unscrew it, so it popped open and the skin shavings went all over me. Like when you sneeze on a powdered-sugar donut. It got on my face and lips. I breathed some of it in. I was in the bathroom, hopping from foot to foot, trying to figure out how to decontaminate myself. She was in the bedroom saying, "J-a-a-ames, I've got another foot, ya know."

After that, I couldn't kiss her feet anymore.

Same thing happened to all her other body parts. Her ribcage, her elbows, her hips, her butt—one by one, they devolved into individual dermatological concerns. After six months of zit and fungus and ingrown-hair patrol, I started losing interest.

Trent Gleason would check in with me periodically.

I told him once, "Things are going just fine, Gleason. My god, you're such a vulture."

He said, "Well, vultures can tell when something's about to die."

He's quick that way. Prick.

Funny thing is, Bridget was ready to move the relationship forward. Not the boyfriend-girlfriend relationship—I mean the semi-medical, X-Acto knife, foot-smoothing relationship. It was a victim-of-my-own success kind of situation. She made me operate on her ingrown toenail so she could ride in some bike race for charity.

I said, "I really think you need a doctor for this kind of thing."

She laughed. "Just cut me open, lover."

After a while she started asking me questions I couldn't handle.

"Hey James, my pee kinda smells like dish soap. What do you suppose that means? C'mere and smell. Think something's wrong with my bladder?"

It's not that I'm a wuss. I've worked on my lady with an X-Acto knife. I'm not squeamish, but our physical intimacy became bodily intimacy. Those are two different things. That's why a woman can sit on that table with the stirrups while a stranger gives her a pelvic exam. It's not exciting; it's clinical. That's how I thought about her: as my patient. Sometimes, instead of sex, I'd just loofah her knees and heels, maybe give her a quick breast exam. I didn't know whether to smoke a cigarette or bill her insurance.

I finally told her: "I can't do this anymore. We can't stay together."

That went over about like you'd think. It was like her ingrown toenail. She was crying, blood everywhere. That's when I started thinking about what I was doing, about how every relationship I've ever been in had some version of ingrown hairs and infected toenails. Something I'd put up with for a while and then just drop.

With Chloe it was watching chick flicks all the time and pretending I liked them. With Katy it was all the clean eating and pretending it made me feel better.

When Chloe moved in, I said we could get a puppy, but then I just stalled until we broke up. I told Katy I'd do yoga with her every day and I made it about two days before I quit.

I told Bridget the same thing about her charity races and volunteer stuff.

"Yeah, babe. Sure. I'll help you."

Never helped her.

I mean, what's worse? Having a big nasty zit on your shoulder that needs popping, or saying you'll do volunteer stuff knowing for a fact you won't?

So, she was crying and I was waffling, thinking maybe we could start over with some ground rules. But she was already cut open and draining. All I could do was mop it up, try to at least keep it sterile and do better with the next girl.

Trent Gleason didn't waste any time. Bridget wasn't even completely moved out when he texted me: *was gonna stop by and check out your new place ok*

I'd been living there for months already. He didn't give two shits about my "new place" and he was the very last goddam person on earth I wanted to see. I was lying on the bed when I got the text. Some of Bridget's things were still around. Sweater on the chair, hand lotion on the vanity, her smell. I guess I'm saying I finally understood why her old boyfriends called. Guys from back in college, from high school even.

But it was too late for me. You can't unlance a boil, can't unpeel a sunburn.

sure man come over any time

I almost added, *hey btw trent ive lived here almost 7 mo and just wanted to let you know i hate your goddamn guts*, but of course he already knew all that.

He didn't act arrogant. I give him credit for that. The Rangers were playing that night and he watched the game with me. He never was such a bad guy, and he knows hockey. When the Rangers were up by two, he took a sip of Dr. Pepper and said, "Sooo, I hear you and Bridget are through."

I said, "Yes, we are."

He said, "I was thinking of asking her out. Unless you're not cool with it, unless you think things would, you know, get messy."

I didn't say a word. I just got up from the couch and walked out. He sat there. I went in the bathroom and got the Little Black Bag. I unzipped it and looked inside. There were a few things I'd added: surgical gloves, a better pair of tweezers. I'd gotten one of those little mirrors dentists use—I'm not even going to explain that one. I zipped it all up, went back to the couch, and handed the bag to Trent.

He opened it, took out the foot smoother, the X-Acto knife. He said, "What's all this for?"

"It's for her," I said. "It's all for her."

HOW BAD IT'S GOTTEN

Let me tell you how bad it's gotten.

The other day at the office I was filling out my W-4 packet. We have to fill it out at the beginning of every year—how much to withhold for taxes, how much for retirement, for medical. Big packet. So I go to Accounting and get last year's packet, and I put the old forms and the new ones side-by-side on my desk. They tell me I can do it on the computer nowadays, but I'm a paper-and-pencil guy. So. I'm going to copy the information from the old forms to the new forms.

Now. Eighteen years I've worked there, eighteen years I've been filling out these forms, but this time I put my pencil in the space for my last name and it just sits there.

This is how bad it's gotten.

I'm thinking, go ahead, start writing. Nothing. So, I look over at the old form and I see the first letter of my last name and my brain kicks in. Like my old lawnmower—once it got started it was fine, once I got a good pull on that rope, but I'm thinking, Jiminy H. Christmas, did I just have to cheat to write down my own last name?

It reminded me of doing a crossword puzzle. All I needed was the first letter. I do a lot of crosswords. I do woodworking, too. Cabinetmaking. I like golf. It's all stuff that supposedly keeps the mind sharp. So I get those little crossword magazines at the drugstore or the airport and I do them on the plane and at the doctor's office. My kids put a program on my tablet with something like a zillion crosswords on it, but it's just not the same. That crackle of the paper. The scratching of the pencil lead. I like that. And I like the magazines full of puzzles better than doing the ones in the newspaper because you get fifty, sixty crosswords, rather than only one a day—not to mention newspapers are getting harder and harder to find.

Plus, when you get the little books, all the answers are right there in the back.

It's not that I cheat—I try really hard not to cheat, which is stupid, I know, because who cares? If I cheat on a crossword, no one on that plane is going to say anything. They won't even see. But this is how far I've sunk. I look up the answers more and more nowadays, and I feel like everyone's watching me to see if I do. So, if anyone's looking in my direction, I won't look up that answer. I'll tap my chin with the pencil, like I'm thinking hard, but I'm really waiting for them to look away. Then I'll flip to the back of the book, look up the answer. And I do it real fast so I don't get caught. And I'm good at it.

That's how bad it is now.

I like pencils. I don't use pens. I know a lot of people who do crosswords in ink, and they'll let you know it, too, like it makes them some kind of super-genius. Come on. It's a crossword. Tell me why my diverticulitis keeps coming back even though I haven't eaten french fries or onion rings or popcorn at the movies in two years—then I'll give you the Nobel Prize. Until then, I'm using a pencil. I'm not ashamed. I've used them all my life. Good old number-two Eberhard Fabers. Helen keeps a cup of sharp ones on my desk at home, and Judy keeps a cup full for my desk at work. Nothing like the smell of a freshly sharpened pencil, and I'll be honest with you—I need that eraser. Like I said, I'm getting the words wrong all the time nowadays.

The other day there was a four-letter word for "Comes out of a radiator." First letter: H. Couldn't get it. Could—not—get it. I had that first letter and I still couldn't get it. I'm thinking, antifreeze? steam? water? It's *heat*, obviously. Easy. But I was thinking of the radiator in a car, and nothing's supposed to come out of your radiator unless it's leaking, unless it's broken. I didn't even think of a heater, even though that's what we had to keep us warm when I was a kid—radiators in every room. But it's like my brain has gotten crusted over and it can't turn and go off in a different direction if it needs to. And here I've still got a few years to retire. I've got to fill out this W-4 packet two more times.

So but then it's time to fill in the space for my first name. Same thing: hand just lays there. I can practically feel the signals coming down from my brain and into the nerves that go into my arm and my wrist, but then they just stop. Nothing goes any further.

The old form is saying, "C'mon, take a peek! Just the first letter!" I say, "No. No way am I looking at the old form."

I'm a pretty smart guy. I didn't get where I am by

being stupid. Retired from the Air Force as a major and I've worked as a cost analysis contractor for the Department of Defense since then. The other day there was a fifteen-letter word, and the clue was, "Granddad said it wasn't so great." I got it right off the bat, no letters filled in. *Great Depression.* Two words, fifteen letters. Not everyone could get a clue like that with no letters filled in, but I did. Two days later I can't write my own name without looking up the answer.

You know what I think it is? The quiet. It gets so quiet in that office. I read in a newspaper somewhere that there's an experimental room in some laboratory in Minnesota that is so quiet, you can hear not just your own heart beating but the blood flowing through your veins. It's so quiet in there that you can't stay inside for more than an hour without going actually insane. That's how it is in my office these days. It's like you can't form a thought because there's nothing to anchor to. Sometimes I feel like I really can hear my own blood and that I really am going insane.

And the seconds are ticking by. That's the big problem—I feel time passing, passing, passing. When you're trying to remember something like that, every second seems like an hour, or an entire day. This is not, "Where did I put my keys?" This is, "What is my name? How do I spell it?"

No one ever says my name at home. I'm not saying I need someone to say my name to remember what it is, but I'm just saying it's a word I sometimes don't hear very often. Helen calls me "Hon" or "Sweetie." My son calls me "Pop," but the grandkids call Helen "Mee-ma" and they call me "Pee-pa." I don't know where they came up with that—from their mother, maybe. I'll be honest with you—if you walked up to me on the sidewalk and called me Pee-pa, I'd kick you right *in* your pee-pa. You know what we called my grandfather? *Grandfather.* That's what he was: a grand father. I'd love it if they called me that, but these are little kids. They're gonna call you whatever they want.

My hand is just sitting there with the pencil, like it's paralyzed, like it's gone dead. And so I feel like my only hope is that someone walks by my office and says, "Hey, *Val.* How you doing, *Val?* Let's go hit some golf balls, *Val.*"

When I first joined the firm we didn't call each other by our first names. It was strictly last names, and "mister" for supervisors. Mr. Clark, Mr. Johnson, just like in the Service. These new guys, the junior analysts, they use first names for everyone—hey Mike, hey Lance. And they got nicknames like "Boomer" and "Slice." I'll be honest—I never approved of it, but now I'm praying one of them walks by and says my name.

That would not be cheating. If someone walked by and said, "Hi, Val," that is definitely not cheating. It'd be like the other day when I got stuck on a crossword and I said, "Hey, Helen, remind me—what's the capital of Norway?" That wasn't cheating because I knew the capital of Norway at one time, I just couldn't think of it right then. So that's not cheating, right? The crossword is testing to see if you know the word, and I did. It's not a memory test. So when Helen says "It's Oslo," I'm not gonna say, "Oh, really? Interesting," I'm gonna say, "Right, right. Oslo. Of course."

But I can't poke my head out of my office and say, "Hey, Judy, remind me—what's my very own first name?" I know I'm on my own, and it's just so quiet.

Maybe Helen's right. Maybe it's not really that quiet and I've just gone deaf. But the phones don't even ring nowadays. Everyone uses the e-mail; they just go on their computer or they text on their phones. Nobody talks anymore, nobody calls. It's dead silent.

Now I'm thinking, which is worse? Waiting thirty seconds to remember my name, or copying it like some kind of cheater? Let's be honest—there's no good answer to that question. They're both worse.

I finally pawned the whole thing off on Judy. I don't know what I told her—something about I couldn't read the small print, didn't have time. This is how bad it's gotten—I get these foggy days like this, where I pawn it all off on Judy. I hope I didn't need to make any big decisions this year, like because of some big change in the taxes, because I told her to just copy everything exactly from the old forms to the new ones and give it back to Accounting.

Then I got out of there. I fled the scene.

And sure enough, that is when I see the young guys, over by McDade's office, looking at something on his computer, laughing. They never have enough to do. I make a beeline for the elevators but I as I pass by McDade's office door, the guys see me.

"Hey, Val," they say. "Hey, how you doing, Val? Hey, let's go golfing, Val."

I'm thinking, thanks for nothing, you guys. I get in the elevator. But the young guys are fast. They catch me up. McDade sticks his arm out so the door can't shut.

They say, "Val, you all right? Where you going? You're looking kind of pale."

I tell them, "No, it's fine, just getting something to eat," but when the doors finally shut I start pulling off my tie like it's trying to strangle me.

The elevator sinks down. I'm breathing hard. It's quiet. It's not even eleven and I'm practically running out to lunch. I shove the front doors open, turn, go down the sidewalk. The air is cool. It's a nice day. Sunny. I get to the coffee place and all the people there have got their noses in their little phones or their computers, punching the keys, but it's noisy in the coffee place. It's loud. I start settling down.

The gal at the cash register says, "Heya, Val. Going with the usual today?"

"Yeah," I say. "Going with the usual today."

She fills up the cup, puts a lid on it. Napkin. Straw. She hands me the cup.

Here's the thing: I've never seen this gal before. I don't know her, and I have no idea what "the usual" is. No idea at all.

This is how bad it's gotten.

BRING THE JACKETS

I'm still in my nightgown, but Terry's got the car almost packed. I make some coffee and sit at the kitchen table and watch him through the front window. He's made about twenty trips so far. Sometimes he takes just one thing out to the car. Like just the water jug. Other times he takes a big armload and drops stuff on the driveway as he goes. A couple times he goes out and brings something back into the house. It's slow going. He must have gotten up at six.

Terry props open the front door using Mazy's Big Wheel as a doorstop. He takes out the folding chairs, then trips over the Big Wheel on his way back in. He gathers up another big armful and stops at the kitchen. He's carrying our big, red-and-white ice chest with my beachbag perched on top.

Peeking around the beachbag, he says, "Babe, want me to grab you a jacket?"

I wish. Two or three hours of rain is all we'd need for an excuse to stay home, but the sky is spotless blue. Disgusting, spotless blue.

"Look outside, Ter," I say waving at the sky, peering

up out of the kitchen window. "What makes you think anyone's gonna need a jacket?"

"Supposed to be windy and cold up there later."

It's not even eight in the morning and he's sweating already. His glasses slide down to the tip of his nose. He scrunches his face to keep them from falling completely off.

"Hon, it's almost ninety out there already. Not once in eight years have ever we needed jackets."

"So, want me to bring 'em?"

"Sure, babe. Bring the jackets. Bring your mittens, while you're at it."

He continues to the car and throws his weight behind the cooler to cram it into the hatchback, but he bangs his head on the edge of the car. The beachbag falls, and my books and sunglasses spill out. Terry rubs his head and checks for blood, then bends down to pick up my things. His butt cheeks and asscrack emerge, radiant in the perfect sunlight.

Usually, I'm the one prodding him to get ready. If anyone has a right to hate my family's camping trip, it's Terry. He's the one my brothers pick on. He's the one who gets de-pants'ed or shoved in the water.

My dad won't do anything about it. One year I said, "Dad, you gotta do something about Brian and Derek. Tell them to lay off Terry."

Mom said, "She might be right, Bill. They're awful hard on him."

Dad said, "Ah, you two don't get it. You can't do it that way. If I tell them to lay off Terry, they'll know they're getting to him. It'd be blood in the water."

"Then what are we supposed to do?" I asked. "How are we supposed to come for Christmas or go camping when they're constantly hiding his inhaler or putting food in his shoes?"

"They hide his inhaler?"

Mom and I nod.

Dad takes a deep breath and lets it out slowly. "Well, Kell, this isn't gonna sound fair, but it's gotta come from him. He's gotta find his place and, you know, stake it out. Defend it."

I know he's right. I just didn't want to hear it. At Christmas, Thanksgiving, and the camping trip—at every big family thing—I feel a heavy little rock form in my stomach, and it's made out of the things Dad just said.

I'm not sure how things got turned around, but at least this year it's Terry who's pushing to get on the road, so at least I don't have to pack, and at least Terry's gotten Mazy up and dressed. He's eager to get it over with, I guess, or maybe he doesn't care anymore.

He comes back into the kitchen and says, "All packed."

I look out the kitchen window and say, "Great. Let's go." And then I look at my phone again and take a sip of coffee.

By then Terry's so sweaty he has to change his t-shirt, jiggling all over as he pulls a fresh one over his belly. He's picked his favorite one—black with a white line drawing like a blueprint of the new military jet, the one that costs a bazillion dollars.

"When are you going to get ready?" he puffs as he combs his hair down.

I put down my phone. I watch him for a few seconds, then say, "What if we didn't go?"

"Didn't go to where?"

"Camping," I say. "What if we just—didn't go?"

"You mean what if we just—didn't go?"

"Yeah."

"Just not show up."

"Yeah. It's just a camping trip," I say with an exaggerated shrug. "We could stay here and you could make us something on the grill."

"You don't like it when I grill," says Terry. "You say it's burnt on the outside and raw on the inside."

He's right. "We'll go out, then."

"Nah," he says, "your family'd kill us. You even said so. Why don't you wanna go?"

"I dunno. Derek and Brian can be such jerks."

He waves his hand. "I just ignore them."

"Derek pushed you in the lake last year. You just about lost your inhaler."

"No, that was two years ago," says Terry. "Last year all he did was put ambrosia in my Crocs. And sleeping bag."

"That's what I mean. They're such jerks."

He widens his eyes a little and shakes his head slowly. "We can't just not show up. 'Sides, you're gonna wanna talk to your mom. Mazy's been dying to see the cousins. And we gotta get moving if we want a good spot."

He's right again. He goes down the hall and calls Mazy. I get in the shower.

When I was a kid, I couldn't wait for the trip. It's not exactly a family reunion, although my Uncle Ricky rides his motorbike over from New Mexico and halfway across Texas to be there. Never misses it. A lot of Mom's family comes, too, but it's also old family friends, work friends, people I don't even know. It's where I learned to swim, where I first kissed a boy. Back in those days we'd play so hard we'd end up asleep in the back of my dad's old truck well before the first of the fireworks exploded out over the lake.

After I shower, I go into the bedroom and sit on the bed, still wearing my robe, thinking of all the things that wouldn't happen if we didn't go—the pranks, the taunts, the awkward backing down. Then I thought of the things we could do instead—take a nap, sit in the backyard, read. Mazy could run in the sprinkler, her panties wet and sagging. Terry could light sparklers for us.

Out in the driveway Terry gives the horn a couple quick toots to keep me moving. I dry my hair, get dressed. I put on a sleeveless collared shirt with stripes which I think somehow makes me look a little less chubby. When I come out, Terry opens the car door for me. He's got the AC blasting. I slump into the passenger seat. Mazy's fastened into the car seat with her Speak & Spell.

"Seatbelt, Mommy," she says.

"Okay, sweetie, thanks."

I buckle up, eyeing Terry as he hustles around to the driver's side. He gets in and we back out and get on the street.

"Seatbelt, Daddy," Mazy says.

He puts on his seatbelt as we take a corner, and we just about sideswipe Mrs. Shultz in her Oldsmobile.

"Slow down, hon, jeeze," I say.

"Yeah, hon, jeeze," says Mazy.

Terry eases up, but it seems like he's leaning forward, like it'll make us go faster. I watch him as we pass by the front yards and cul de sacs. He's grinning a little, but with the same expression he gets when he finally decides to jump off the high-dive at the city pool.

"What?" I ask him. "What's with you?"

He shrugs. "I'm just excited. Sometimes it's just good to get out."

We drive through town and get on the frontage road. He's definitely leaning forward, definitely grinning.

"Have you got some sort of plan?" I ask. "Are you gonna to try to pull something on my brothers?"

Terry looks at the speedometer for no reason. He swings onto the highway and floors it.

"You can't beat them, Ter. Derek'll see you coming from a mile away. From two miles."

Terry glances over, shows me the grin.

"Oh, you are planning something. This is so not-a-good idea."

The prospect of Terry making a move against Derek seems to lighten the weight in my stomach, makes the rock down there less dreadful. That Terry would finally do something, that he would stick up for himself gives me a queasy feeling of hope. But then I picture Terry trying to prank Derek or even stand up to him, and how that might play out, and then the rock feels heavier.

Terry says, "I just want to get there, okay? We gotta get there if we want a good spot."

He's right about that. Dad reserved the whole huge camping area again this year, but if we're late we'll have to camp down by the water with the mosquitoes, or up on the hillside where everything's slanted. We want to be down by the big firepits.

I quiz Terry about what he packed.

Terry hands me his phone. "Here," he says. "Open the first checklist."

I scroll through the list. It's everything I'd pack, and a few things I'd have forgotten, like the marshmallow sticks and bug spray. It's a good list, and I'm getting ready to send it to myself for later reference when I see the last item.

Kite.

I look up from the phone. "Wait. The kite? You brought the kite?"

He looks at the speedometer.

The kite is a sensitive subject. It's not a regular kite like from the supermarket. It's a special stunt kite, and Terry put it on our credit card without telling me. This was five or six years ago, before we had Mazy, before Terry started working at Barr-Kane. It cost a lot of money, and we didn't have a lot of money.

I knew why he wanted it. I know why he loves it. See, not very many people get to be exactly what they want to be in life, and that's too bad. But some people want to be the one thing they can never be, and that's Terry. He wanted to be a fighter pilot. Or any kind of pilot for that matter. He loves jets, knows every single thing about them, but he's got so many health issues he never had a prayer of going into the military, let alone getting close to any jets.

Terry's mom once told me, "The Air Force recruiter wouldn't even give him a free t-shirt."

Terry's a great programmer. I think he likes his job. He says he does. But get him close to any airplane and he gets a look in his eyes. Like a kid seeing the only Christmas present he wants, knowing he'll never get it. So, I let him keep the kite. Grudgingly.

The lake would be a great place to fly it, too, but Terry knows I don't like to even look at the thing. Since then he's bought remote-control planes and a drone— also without asking—but he always comes back to his kite, like it's his first true love, and it's still one of the few things we fight about. He has to go to a park on the other side of town to fly it. He's in a kite club with his buddies and they all fly their kites together for hours—

without wives, without kids. They buy things for their kites, pamper them. They take pictures and videos of them to post online.

"I get it now," I say. "You're gonna be off flying your kite the whole time."

"No. Not the whole time."

"That's how you're gonna *ignore* Derek and Brian."

"No, no," he says. "It's not that."

"And I'll be stuck talking to Cherise and Shaylyn. I hate that kite."

"No, hon, that's not it. You've never even seen me fly," says Terry. "I'm one of the best in the club now. Josh even said so."

As if bringing Josh into this is going to help at all. Josh, the licensed pilot. Josh, president of the Kite Boy Club. He orders them around and they all want him to tell them they're good at flying kites and drones and toy helicopters.

"Mazy's excited to see me fly. Right, sweetie?"

Mazy hides her face with her arm and says, "I'm not diposta say anything about it to Mommy."

"Mommy knows about it now," says Terry.

"Favorite shirt," I say. "Getting up early. Packing the car. I get it."

Terry clams up, but he speeds the rest of the way, so we are at least nice and early. The campground is a big grassy area that wraps around a quiet cove on the north end of the lake. There's a wall of big cottonwoods on one side and brushy hills on the other. Down by the shore there's a sandy beach between the willow trees.

Mom and Dad come and greet us at the car. We all hug, and my mom takes Mazy and kisses her all over her face. Dad helps us carry our camp chairs.

"Where you want me to set these down, Ter?" says

Dad.

Derek isn't there yet, so the space next to my dad's camp trailer by the big firepit is wide open.

"I dunno," says Terry. "You think Derek will care if we set up right next to you?"

My dad shrugs and sets the chairs down. "He'll get over it. He knows to get here early. Like you guys did. You set up where you want, Terry." He and my mom go and sit in their camp chairs beneath the blue-and-white-striped awning of their trailer.

Terry smiles. He starts putting up our tent, right there next to the trailer. The big firepit will be right outside the front door. He hammers the tent stakes, assembles the poles. His ass crack shows as he bends and squats.

The sun climbs higher in the clear hot sky. More people show up, and pretty soon Mazy is swept away by a herd of cousins. They go to the water to throw rocks, the same rocks I threw when I was little. There's no wind, and the water is so smooth that the rings expand way out into the lake, like they could travel to the other side.

"I wonder where Derek is," says Terry.

My parents shrug in unison. I unfold a chair and sit by them. They both sit exactly the same way—slumped down, ankles crossed, arms draped over the armrests. King and queen of the campground. Terry sits on the ground. He pulls up a clump of grass, holds it in the air, and drops it—checking for wind—but the blades of grass fall straight to the ground.

A little after lunchtime, Derek swings into the campground in his enormous Chevy truck. It glitters with so much chrome my mom shades her eyes to look at it. We can the hear music inside the truck thumping all the way across the campground. Behind the Chevy is a trailer with two jet-skis.

"What an outfit," says Dad. He shakes his head at the excess of it, but there's an undertone of admiration in his voice.

"Hurts my eyes," says Mom.

The kids hoard around as Derek dismounts his truck, even though they know it will probably be tomorrow before he gives them any jet-ski rides.

Derek towers above even the tallest of the cousins, and he's wider than any two of them. He's wearing a tight, red-and-white-striped rugby shirt. He looks the place over as if he just conquered it. Cherise hops out of the passenger side. Her huge sunglasses hide everything but the tip of her nose and her mouth.

Brian arrives a few minutes later. His truck is smaller than Derek's but just as loud and shiny. He gets out. Same rugby shirt, but with blue strips. He and Derek grab each other and wrestle. The kids back away. It's like watching a buffalo fight with a bear. Pretty soon Brian's in a chokehold. His face turns purple before Derek lets him go.

Shalyn gets out of Brian's truck and finds her place next to Cherise. They mince through the grass in their high-heeled sandals like they're afraid they'll step in something vile.

"Benny," Cherise warns one of the cousins who's running at her for a hug, "don't you dare put those muddy paws on me."

The two wives look almost alike. The same big sunglasses, the same crisp, pale clothes. Shalyn is shorter than Cherise, and she's skinny, but not as skinny as Cherise. No one can be as skinny as Cherise. They come over and dispense hugs on Mom and Dad without really touching them.

"How are you two doing?" asks Cherise. "Me and Derek have been meaning to come by. You guys getting around okay?"

Mom and Dad look at each other.

"Getting around what?" says Mom.

Shalyn stays quiet and stands with her arms folded. She's been in the family for a few years, but she's still the newest daughter-in-law, and so she rarely speaks unless spoken to. She keeps adjusting the way her bangs lay across her forehead, as if it's the one thing she can do without permission from Cherise.

Cherise touches Mom's arm and says, "Tell me you brought your fried chicken."

"Sure, dear," says Mom. "You want a piece?"

"Oh, no," she says. She pats her flat, featureless tummy, as though that explains her answer. "But I have got to get that recipe."

I can't help myself. I say, "Cherise, you cook?"

Cherise fake-laughs. Dad laughs for real, then fake-coughs to take it back. Mom shoots me a look. Terry watches all of this like a foreign national observing an unsettling indigenous ritual.

"Kelly," coos Cherise. She minces over to me. "Lookit you, girl. I can see why you always wear that shirt." She leans in for the no-touch hug and says in a whisper loud enough for everyone else to hear: "It really slims you down."

Derek and Brian set up a couple camp chairs in the shade for Cherise and Shalyn, and the two wives leave us, thumbing their phones as they go.

Then Derek comes toward us carrying his tent. It's a big cabin tent, but it's tucked under his arm like a rolled-up newspaper. When I was a kid, I thought I knew Derek and all my brothers and sisters really well. I lived with them, ate with them, shared beds with them. Derek was my favorite—I thought he was a happy, big-hearted kid. When we moved out, I thought I wouldn't know him so well anymore because we'd only see each other a few times a year. But in some ways I got to know him better. The infrequent contact allowed me to see him the way other people saw him, and I understood why some people never liked him. Or were afraid of him.

Derek looks at our tent, then Dad's camper, then Terry.

Terry sits still. Derek throws down his tent and it lands on the grass with a loud *whump*.

"Terry, why'd you put your tent right here?"

Before Terry reacts, Dad says, "It's called camping, son. Perhaps the concept is foreign to you."

Terry stifles a laugh.

"But why right here?" huffs Derek. "If they move it ten feet that way, me and Bry can put our tents in here, too. They're hogging all the room."

"We got the whole campground," says Dad. "How much room do you need?"

Derek snorts and glares at Terry. Terry looks away, and I should be embarrassed for him, and I should maybe even say something, but I stay quiet.

Dad points across the campground. "There's some nice spots over there by Ricky's firepit."

"I don't wanna sleep by Ricky. He snores."

"So do you, sweetie," chirps Mom.

"Fine." Derek scoops up his big tent. "Damn waste of space, though," he says, glaring at Terry once more.

"Language," says Mom.

"We're camping over by Ricky," Derek yells at Brian. "Too crowded over here."

"See that, Kelly?" says Dad. "Blood in the water."

Derek opens a beer and recruits some kids to set up his tent for him. He heckles and trips them while they work. Brian sets up his own tent and Derek trips and heckles him, too.

When the tents are set up, Derek shucks his shirt and backs the jet-ski trailer down the gravelly beach. Brian follows suit. The jet-skis float free and they climb on. The kids crowd along the shore and watch Derek and Brian circle the cove and gun the engines. Brian turns for open water, but Derek races straight at the shore and the kids. When he's only twenty feet out, he turns hard and sprays them all with a sheet of water. Then he's gone, too. The kids stand dripping and listening to the receding growl of the machines out on the lake.

Terry heads for the car and he's back in one minute. The kite comes in its own duffel sack, and he's got a special backpack for the controls and spools of string and spare parts. He lays out everything out in an open area, away from the tents. He looks at the kids, but they're still down at the shoreline.

The kite's got lots of little carbon-fiber braces and tubes. Terry unfolds the black wings like he's reviving a huge, sleepy bat. It's as wide as he is tall.

"What's he got over there?" says Dad.

I sigh. "It's his kite."

Mom says, "Oh, so that's the kite."

Dad says, "Looks like a hang glider."

A couple kids spot Terry and watch him, from a distance at first, then they move closer. Mazy runs over, even though Terry tells her all the time that she can't touch the kite. Terry positions the kite and trails the strings across the grass. A few more kids go over to see.

"But there's hardly any wind," says Mom.

"That kind of kite doesn't need much wind," I tell her wearily. "It's a special kind of kite."

Terry motions the kids to move away from the kite and the strings.

He says, "Please don't step on the lines, okay you guys?"

Benny stomps on them and then runs off. The rest of the kids stick around, maintaining a respectful distance. They're excited now. Terry props the kite into a kind of sitting position, with its nose pointed skyward. Then he stands there for a few seconds with his head down. As if what he will do next is important. He puts his earbuds in his ears and starts a song on his phone. Then he picks up the black control handles. They're like marionette paddles, only styled kind of like a pilot's controls. In step to the beat no one else can hear, Terry pulls the controls sharply and shuffles backwards. His belly jiggles, but his movements are somehow graceful and steady. The kite lifts fifty feet straight into the air. The kids cheer.

My mouth drops open a little.

"Would you look at that," says Dad.

There is a faint breeze, and when Terry yanks one of the handles, the kite peels off to one side. I knew it was a stunt kite, but I'd never imagined it moved with such precision. The turn is sharp, crisp. Terry yanks the other handle and the kite goes the other way. The kids run around with upturned faces and arms reaching skyward.

The breeze gusts a little and cools the sweat on our necks. Just that little bit of wind lets Terry put on a show. The kite soars high, stalls, then plunges down and almost hits the ground before turning up and soaring again. Terry can even make it land on the ground on its wingtips. The kids chase it but he makes it dart into the air again. They squeal and clap.

Terry looks over his shoulder at me. Even through his glasses I can see his eyes blaze deliriously. I give him a little wave and he tilts back his head and laughs like a school kid.

This goes on for a couple hours, with a few intermissions. Terry lets some of the kids hold the controls. I catch up with Mom and Dad, but we stop and clap a lot for the good tricks. Just about everyone is watching, too. Even Cherise and Shalyn glance up from their phones from time to time.

"I like it when it looks like it's gonna crash but then he saves it at the last second," says Mom.

"I like when it does a figure-eight," says Dad.

Something is happening out on the lake. Hot air colliding with wet air, or maybe cool air hitting dry. Terry could describe the phenomenon more accurately, but a line of billowy clouds with grey underneath gathers over the south side of the lake. There's a cool, steady breeze coming in now and waves march into shore.

"Those boys oughta be getting back," says my dad flipping up his sunglasses and looking at the water. "Getting choppy."

The wind is chilly on my bare arms, but with the stiffer breezes, Terry can make the kite turn front-to-back and whirl in endless corkscrews. His face is red and he's breathing hard. He jumps over the kite strings and holds the handles behind his back. Uncle Ricky pushes his cowboy hat back on his head, removes his mirrored shades, and shakes his head in unveiled amazement. The kids have their chairs set up like an audience. They munch on their pretzels and fruit snacks. Almost nobody notices when Derek and Brian bounce over the waves into the cove and glide to shore. No kids mob them, no one asks for a ride.

The boys dry off and change clothes, then come up from the beach, puzzled, inspecting. No one but me seems to notice them. Everyone's watching the angular black creature swoop and dip in the sky. Terry brings the kite low enough for the kids to pet it. He holds the kite almost motionless just a few feet off the ground.

The kids touch it fast and jerk their hands back like it's a wild, living thing. They run away squealing and Terry hoists the kite higher, where it spins and crackles.

Derek and Brian smirk at the spectacle. They get out a football and try to draft Uncle Ricky and the other adults into a game. But not even the kids are interested. So they play catch by themselves, but they watch Terry and his kite.

Dad points at the kite and says, "Oh, didja see that one?" but I catch him sneaking glances at the boys and their football. I'm doing the same.

Derek motions for Brian to go long. Brian sneers and they nod to one another. Brian runs toward Terry, jumps over some seated kids, and when he's almost under the kite, Derek launches the football.

The ball rockets directly at the kite. At first I figure it's way too far away to hit, but the wind carries the ball beyond even Derek's throwing range, and we all gasp as one when the ball smacks into the kite like a missile.

The kite falters. Something has snapped, one wing droops and flaps. Then the kite wheels over and dives noisily into the grass. It comes down nose first and flutters there like a wounded pterodactyl.

Terry whips around to see where the football came from. Everyone does. All eyes go to Derek. He stands there grinning in his rugby shirt, arms folded across his chest. A groaning chorus of disapproval rises above the wind. Derek shrugs and laughs.

"It was an accident," he shouts, spreading his arms.

I turn to my dad and say, "Dad, would you please do something?"

Dad is sitting up in his chair, like he's watching a big play unfold in a football game. He holds up one finger, narrows his eyes, and watches Terry.

Terry kneels at the crash site. His hair blows around in the wind. He takes out his headphones and examines the great, injured bird. The kids circle around him.

"Is it broken?" says Mazy.

Terry turns the kite over, laying it out in the grass. He fiddles with one of the braces.

"Is it killed?" says Mazy.

"Nah," says Terry. "It's just fine."

When the kite rushes up into the wind again, the whole campground roars. It loops up and up, triumphant. The kids shout and hoot. Derek stands in the grass with his arms folded, shaking his head. My dad settles back into his chair, but his eyes dart from Terry to Brian to Derek.

Then the kite turns and begins to cross the campground. I look down, and Terry's on the move. He walks the kite over by Derek, then stops and holds the kite ten feet above Derek's head. Derek scoffs and moves to one side. So does the kite. He moves and the kite follows, like a little raincloud. Everyone laughs.

I laugh, too, but my heart sinks a little. It occurs to me that I've always been concerned about Derek humiliating Terry. I'd never thought of the opposite thing happening.

Terry tightens his grip on the handles and then

makes a move that looks a little like kung fu. The kite inverts and then rips down from the sky, directly at Derek. As it swoops past him, Derek loses his composure, ducking and batting at the kite as it bears down. He stumbles and rolls in the grass as the kite swoops past him. In the stiffening wind, the kite's nylon skin crackles like a machine gun. Derek gets up and staggers along. Terry stalks him with the kite.

Then Derek gets his hands on the football and launches it. He manages a glancing blow to the kite, but it stays airborne. Derek dodges another kite attack, gets the ball, and throws again, but the kite's directly above him. He can't throw straight up.

And we watch. There's a bit of nervous laughter, but mostly we just watch. Dad's up out of his chair again. Mom's hands are tented over her mouth.

Derek tries to approach Terry, but Terry tugs at the lines and the kite screams across Derek's path, only a foot or so from his face. The battle goes on, Derek advancing, Terry keeping him at bay with the kite, but backing up a few steps at a time until they're almost at the water.

We're all out of our chairs and heading down to the shore. I pick up Mazy on the way there.

"Bring it down here," growls Derek, panting, gripping the football. "Give me a clean shot, I dare ya. Gimme a clean shot and your little playtoy is history."

Terry stands very still, close to the shore, his back to the water, but the lake seems to side with Terry, its continuous breath holding the kite exactly where Terry wants it.

They face each other. Terry works the controls and the kite floats down and holds steady on the wind twenty feet in the air between them, rattling like crazy.

Derek fakes a throw. The kite doesn't move. He fakes again. Terry flinches but holds fast. Then Derek fires the football at the kite and Terry rears back, pulling hard on the lines. The kite leaps up, and the ball flies in a perfect spiral underneath the kite and out over the water, where it spins out against the wind, splashes down, and bobs there on the waves.

Another roar of approval rises from the campground. Uncle Ricky and some of the others have circled around Terry, so he lands the kite in the grass. The kids gather around it.

"Good kite," they say, "nice kite."

Derek skirts the crowd, glowers at the kite, and then comes up from the beach and storms into his tent.

I turn to my dad.

"See that?" he says with a grin.

He returns to his folding throne over by the trailer.

Uncle Ricky asks about the controls.

"If you go like this," explains Terry, "you shorten that line and the kite'll go right. It kind of feels backwards, but you get used it." He passes the handles to Uncle Ricky and walks over to the kite.

Uncle Ricky pushes his cowboy hat down on his head to secure it. Then he plants his boots and grips the handles, as though inadvertently taking flight is a concern. Terry holds the kite up into the wind, lets it go, and it's flying.

"Would you look at that," laughs Uncle Ricky.

Mazy wiggles out of my arms and runs to Terry, pointing to the kite. I follow her and my mom follows me. Terry picks her up to see better.

"You want a turn, sweetie?" Terry asks.

She nods without looking away from the sky. The kite weaves drunkenly through the sky in response to Uncle

Ricky's clumsy commands. His hat blows off and wheels across the open expanse of grass, but he hangs onto the controls.

Terry kisses Mazy on her cheek. "Oh, she's freezing cold," he says.

My arms are covered with goosebumps, too.

"Got cold out here," Mom says, rubbing her arms. "I have a jacket in the trailer that might could fit her."

"That's okay," I say, slipping my arm around Terry's waist. "Terry brought jackets for all of us. We got them in the car."

THE KEY TO THIS WHOLE ENTIRE THING

Dutch invaded the TV room wearing a dress shirt and no pants. Brass-buckled garters stretched his black dress socks midway up his pale, gnarly calfs, and the tails of an undone necktie hung from his neck.

He positioned himself between Brandon and the television, where Brandon's video game of sci-fi combat zoomed and scrolled at manic speeds. Brandon lay on his side on the sofa, as though he had been sitting but had then tipped over. He held a game controller in both hands near his groin, and the plastic buttons clicked softly as he played.

As Dutch buttoned up his shirt, he said, "We'll be back around eleven-thirty, midnight."

"Okay," said Brandon. His thumbs worked furiously on the controller.

Dutch was barrel-chested and thick through the neck. His arms and shoulders were thickly muscled, too, but below the waist he'd gone spindly with his age, and so Brandon managed to keep his eyes on the game by looking between and around Dutch's legs.

"Guess you'll be out all night, too?" asked Dutch.

"Yeah."

"Well, all right then, sit up for a minute, son," said Dutch, fiddling with the cuffs of his sleeves. "I was getting dressed and I happened to think: what's Brandon gonna wear on Tuesday?"

"For what," said Brandon.

"For the interview. What are you gonna wear for the interview on Tuesday?"

"What am I going to wear?" Only his hands moved. "A shirt. You know. Pants."

"No, get something pressed. You never press anything."

Dutch kept track of all the things Brandon never did and always did.

"You always wear shabby clothes, Bran. *Dress to impress.* That's the key. Sit up a minute so I can talk to you. This is a big deal. Barr-Kane's a good company. Good pay, good bennies. You get on there now and you'll be set when you get your degree, so let's do this right."

"Okay," said Brandon. He shifted subtly to better see the television. Something of critical importance was going on right behind Dutch's left knee, but if Brandon showed too much interest, his father would switch off the television and say, "Pry your eyes away from your games for three seconds and listen."

Dutch hyperbolized time by either condensing it to three seconds or protracting it to fifty-thousand years.

"I want you to pick out a nice dress shirt and take it to the cleaners," said Dutch. "Have it pressed. Medium starch. And don't lose the ticket."

"Okay," said Brandon.

Dutch narrowed his eyes. "Better yet: give the shirt to your mother. You listening? Sit up. She'll iron it for you. Forget the cleaners. You'll lose the ticket or you won't pick it up and then we're screwed. Forget the cleaners, you hear?"

"Okay."

"Tell ya what," said Dutch. "Let's do it right now. You'll forget." Dutch went down the hall to Brandon's bedroom, talking over his shoulder. "What color you want? White? You got a nice white one?"

Brandon played his game. Dutch came back with a white shirt and a blue shirt on hangers.

"White or blue?" said Dutch, holding them out in turn, as though Brandon would be otherwise unable to distinguish them.

"Blue," said Brandon.

"Blue? Why blue?"

"Okay, white."

"Yeah, good." Dutch headed for the kitchen. "Blue is for after you get the job. White says, 'I'm in this to win it.' I'll tell your mother to iron this and put some starch in it," he shouted from the kitchen. "That little extra effort, see, that crispness. That's the key to this. You gotta be noticed, gotta stand out. Might be quite a few people interviewing for this thing."

In the kitchen Dutch hung the white shirt on the laundry room door. Brandon did not move. He lay on the sofa working the game controller.

Then, from upstairs, Brandon's mother, Pat, yelled something about what was taking so long.

"Whaddya mean?" Dutch shouted at the ceiling. "I'm waiting on you. I just need to put my tie on. And my pants."

He rifled the kitchen drawer and came up with some paper and a pencil.

"Come on, hon," he shouted as he wrote, "we're

gonna be late."

She yelled something back to him from upstairs.

"I'm leaving a note for your mother to starch this shirt," Dutch called to Brandon. "I'm sticking it to the fridge."

"Why are you telling me?"

"Just—so you'll know," said Dutch. "And don't move it, or she might not see it. People in this house are always moving my notes."

Dutch wrote the note. He fastened it to the fridge with a magnet shaped like a utility van. Then he swung through the TV room with the blue shirt on its hanger and disappeared down the hall to return it to Brandon's bedroom. When he came back he was holding Brandon's black dress shoes.

"What's this?" he asked.

Brandon's eyes flicked from the TV to the shoes and back in less than one second. "My shoes."

"You told me you shined 'em. You didn't shine 'em."

"I know," said Brandon. "I will."

"No. You'll forget. You always do. Preparation, son, that's the key to this whole thing. No one's gonna take you seriously if you walk in looking like some homeless guy. Look at these. They haven't been shined in fifty-thousand years."

"I'll shine 'em."

"When? You'll be gone all night tonight, and then you'll sleep all day tomorrow. You got class on Monday, then homework, then the interview. You only really got two days till this interview."

"That's four days. Saturday-Sunday-Monday-Tuesday."

"It's three days," said Dutch, counting them off on his fingers. "Sunday, Monday, Tuesday."

"You said two days."

"Well, today's over with, and you don't count the day-of, so it *is* two days: Sunday and Monday. Point being, when are you going to shine these?"

"Tomorrow."

"Tell ya what," said his father, tossing the shoes onto the couch, "do it right now. Take you three seconds. Go get my shine kit. I'll wait."

"I don't know where your shine kit is," said Brandon.

"Bottom drawer of my nightstand," said Dutch, as if this were common knowledge.

Only Brandon's hands moved. The controller clicked softly.

"Oh for hell's sake," said Dutch. "I'll get it."

He met Pat just as she descended the staircase in a cloud of hairspray smell. She was what men once characterized as "handsome," which meant she was well-coiffed and well-dressed without being particularly beautiful. Pat's graying hair was dyed expensively brown and her makeup was always tasteful, but she looked mildly bothered at all times. She wore a dark, modest dress, and her shiny patent-leather pumps clopped on the tile.

Without looking at Dutch she passed by and said, "You're ready? You don't look ready. What are you doing now?"

"Gotta get my shine kit," said Dutch as he mounted the stairs.

"You're shining your shoes? Again? Honestly, how shiny do they need to be?" She was pinching and tugging at the dress, adjusting the tightly fastened, overlapping undergarments that held her together.

"No," said Dutch. He walked backward down a few steps and jerked his thumb at the TV room. "I'm gonna shine his shoes." Then he continued up.

"What for?" She centered up her brassiere with a sharp, final tug.

Dutch reversed again and leaned over the bannister. He glanced in the direction of the TV room.

"Pat," he said softly, beckoning her with a head jerk. "I pulled some strings with Rex from Rotary. 'Member him? Tall guy? Sat by us at the Christmas thing."

"His wife had that red coat I liked."

"That's the guy. He's a VP at Barr-Kane. Told me he'd find a place for Bran while he's in school—a desk job, something with the computers. This'll maybe show him he can make it out on his own."

Pat's hand went to her neck and she looked toward the TV room. How many times had they met in the kitchen for quiet, worried talks about Brandon while he sprawled unknowing in front of the television?

"Oh, I don't know, Dutch," said Pat. "He'd have to drive back and forth every day. And he sure didn't like working for Marty that time."

Dutch scowled and waved his hand. "That was a summer job. He was just an errand boy, got off on the wrong foot. This is different—a real job. Something with the computers. Fixing them. He'll love it. Rex said just send him in on Tuesday and they'll put him right to work. It's a great company. Great pay, great bennies."

"Oh, I don't know. He's gone all night as it is. When would he study?"

"I left you a note on the refrigerator," said Dutch, pointing toward the kitchen. "It says to starch Bran's shirt for his interview. The white one." He went up the stairs.

Pat went into the kitchen and took the note from the refrigerator. It read: *Hon, Starch Bran's shirt for his interview. The white one. —Dutch.* She went to the TV room.

"Hey, sweetie," she said, touching Brandon's head. "What's your father up to down here?"

Brandon paused the game. The figures froze. Brandon looked up at his mother and put his index finger like a gun barrel to his temple. Pat's hand rose to her neck. She looked at the note again before slipping it into her shiny black clutch alongside other notes Dutch had left for her.

"Heard he got you a job interview," she said.

Brandon shrugged his shoulders and shook his head, but both motions were almost too subtle even to see. "I'm not working for another one of his buddies."

"He's just trying to help."

Brandon pressed a button on the controller and the figures in the game resumed their weightless, frantic motions. Pat's face was turned in the direction of the TV but she looked through it rather than at it. Dutch came down the stairs and bustled into the TV room with a brown leather case.

"Sit up," said Dutch. "Pry your eyes away from your games for three seconds and sit up." Dutch picked up the TV remote, pointed it at the TV, and the TV went dark. Then he sat on the coffee table across from Brandon, unzipped the leather shine kit, and began to unpack it.

Pat removed a small tube of moisturizer from the clutch and applied a generous layer of the ointment to her hands. For a while, there were only the sounds of clunking shoe polish cans and the wet smearing of the moisturizer.

"You're going to make us late, aren't you?" said Pat.

"This'll take three seconds. Sit up, son. I said, sit up."

Brandon rose with labored movements into a sitting

position.

"Jesus, you move like you got shit in your veins. You heard your mother: you're making us late." Dutch shoved a shoe into Brandon's lifeless hand.

Brandon dabbed the shoe polish with a shred of cotton towel from the kit and gazed at the darkened television as he listlessly applied the polish to the toe-cap of the shoe. Dutch sat spraddle-legged on the coffee table with his arms folded, as if viewing a sporting event.

"Remember how I showed you," said Dutch. "You remember?"

Brandon recited his answer with the weary sing-song of a grade-schooler: "Rub in circles."

"Little circles," his father cried, wincing. "Not just 'rub in circles,' Bran. Polish. In tight, little circles. Smaller the better. Little is the key!"

Brandon swirled the cloth on the shoe.

"Come on, son, put some polish on there," Dutch urged. "You hardly got any."

Pat watched this with the grimace of one who's being forced to observe the amputation of a human limb. Brandon sagged more and moved less with each reprimand. Dutch at last snatched the shoe away.

"Give me this," he snapped. "You always give up so easy. You never try." Dutch slipped the towel over his finger and inscribed the shoe with whorls of polish that glimmered like tiny vinyl records. "There. See that? Little circles."

Brandon pleaded with his mother by looking up at her and running a hand down his face, gripping so tightly that his lower eyelids prolapsed, their wet veiny undersides gaping grotesquely.

"Leave him alone and go put your pants on," cried

Pat. "You're going to make us late. Honestly."

Dutch picked a set reading glasses from his shirt pocket, flicked them open, and perched them on his nose to better admire the shoe.

"Oh, yeah, lookit that," he chuckled. "At Camp Lejeune I used to love pulling late-night guard duty in the barracks because they'd let you shine your boots and clean your rifle all night. Guys'd pay me to shine their boots when I pulled guard duty. Lookit that."

Brandon and his mother watched together bleakly as Dutch retrieved a soft-bristled brush from the kit. He spat a few tiny drops onto the shoe and finessed the brush over the toe-cap until it shone darkly, as though covered in black ink.

"There," Dutch announced, thrusting the shoe into Brandon's face. "Look right there. Like a mirror."

Brandon's distorted reflection loomed in the shoe's glassy surface.

Dutch held the shoe up to the light. "Yeah, you can see yourself, right there," he purred. "That is the key to this whole entire thing."

MR. COOL RANCH

I wish Whitney wouldn't wear such skimpy outfits, but whenever I tell her to put on something decent, she just pops her gum and looks at me with her hang-dog look and says, "Mother, puh-leeze."

Girls never know how much stress they cause.

It's worst when there's men around. They can't stop looking at her, so tall and blonde. It doesn't help that she shows lots of cleavage these days. I did the same thing when I was her age. Sure, I think it's sick when an older guy ogles a high school girl, but there's no way you can stop that. Can you? I don't even know.

So I say, "Whitney, cover up."

And she says, "Mother, puh-leeze."

And I say, "Whitney, put on a sweater."

And she says, "Mother would you not."

The other day when me and Whitney were in the produce section at Walmarts. I was picking out some grapefruits and here came this guy with a cowboy hat and sunglasses. I'm sorry but I got a thing for guys in cowboy hats and sunglasses. And he had a jumbo bag of Doritos in one hand and six-pack of Miller High Life in the other.

At first I thought, now there's a good-looking stranger.

He was tall, kinda lean. I pictured me and him sitting on the tailgate of a truck somewhere, splitting that six of High Life. It'd been a good long time since I split anything with a guy like him. I heard his bottles clinking and his boots on the floor and I imagined us sipping the beer and feeding each other Doritos. They were even Cool Ranch, the same kind I like.

But then I realized he was just staring at Whitney. She was leaning on the shopping cart handle with her little tube top on, and I just knew he was getting a total eyeful. Didn't even try to hide it. You'da thought he had those x-ray vision glasses that used to be in the back of a comic book.

I almost said something right then. Felt guilty about thinking of eating Doritos with him. This guy was my age, but I didn't want to make a whole big scene. Whitney gets so upset when I make a scene. So, I grabbed the grapefruits, the guy walked on past, and me and Whitney went straight in the other direction. I thought that was that, but as soon as we stopped, I heard his clinking bottles and boot heels behind us. He'd done a u-turn and followed me and Whitney into the bakery, over by the cupcakes. This time Whitney was facing away, so he couldn't see down her top, but she was still bending over that cart. She's got these little cutoffs and long legs and that seventeen-year-old butt that defies gravity.

Whatever it was I needed in the bakery, I didn't get it. I jumped in between Whitney and the guy, trying to act natural but block his view at the same time while we went over to dairy. I was hoping he'd get the message, but I saw him again, in front of the cooler where the milk jugs are at. Whitney was oblivious to this whole thing, popping her gum and twirling her hair. So I gave the guy the dirtiest look I knew how, but he just grinned.

Then—get this—he tipped his hat.

I about flipped. I thought, what kind of a sicko is this?

Whitney said, "Can you puh-leeze not get that no-name yogurt this time? It tastes gross."

I said, "Whit, we're going." I tossed the yogurt in the cart, grabbed her arm, and took off for the front.

She said, "Mother, what is with you? We're supposed to get hot dog buns."

"We're going," I said.

"You got the gross yogurt," she said.

"We're going," I growled at her.

We couldn't shake him. Reminded me of one of those scary movies where the killer just keeps getting up. They shoot him, they throw him out the window, hit him with the car, they think he's dead, but then he gets up and he's behind them again. Sure enough, there he was, at the next register over. Ten, fifteen feet away. Still wearing a big, perverted grin, still had his chips and beer.

I was furious. But what could I do? Lookin's not against the law.

He set his things down at the cash register, looking over at us the whole time. I heard the cashier ask him, "Did you find everything you were looking for today?"

He said, "Yes ma'am, I believe I did all right." All respectful, all polite.

Then the kid at my register said, "Is that gonna be all for you today?"

I was just about in tears. I said, "No wonder everybody hates shopping in here—the people you let wander around in this place."

The kid stared at me. Kinda shook his head. He was probably used to people making whole big scenes. Anyway he had no idea what I was talking about. Whitney, on the other hand, was acting about ready to die. I can always tell when Whitney's about ready to die because it's the only time she chews her gum with her mouth shut. I was past caring about that. I stormed out, pushing the cart so fast the wheels started shaking, wobbling. I almost tipped it right over.

Then I realized I'd walked out without my grapefruits. It's a thirty-five minute drive into town, but I wasn't about to go back in for them. We got to the truck, and I threw the groceries inside. I turned around to put the cart away, and there he was, Mr. High Life.

And he was holding my grapefruits.

I finally snapped. I barked at Whitney to get in and start the truck. I grabbed my purse and stuck my hand in it. My pepper spray was in there and I held onto it, inside the purse, with my thumb on the button. Then I walked right up to him. He was taller than I thought. Real tan.

I said, "Hold it right there, Mr. Cool Ranch."

He chuckled and said, "Howdy. You know you forgot these back there."

"I know I did. I don't care about them. You think I didn't see you, you creeper? Following my daughter? Peeking? Looking at her?"

He pulled his sunglasses down to the tip of his nose and looked at me. He had blue eyes. Which figures. They had to be. He looked over at the truck. Whitney hadn't got in like I told her to. She stood there watching us with this look on her face like we were fornicating right in front of her. The guy smiled and waved at her. She waved back.

He sorta snorted and shook his head. Then he said, "I guess you don't give yourself much credit, do ya?"

I said, "What's that supposed to mean?"

He leaned forward with a kind of disappointed look and said, "Lady. It wasn't her I was lookin' at."

"Oh," I thought. "Okay."

I took my thumb off the button.

He handed me the grapefruits.

I told him, "Well. Thanks. I mean, I'm sorry. I mean, when you got a daughter, you do dumb things sometimes. They never know how much trouble they cause."

He took off the sunglasses and slid them in his shirt pocket. He looked at Whitney again and narrowed his eyes a little and nodded. "I got a couple like her myself. One a little older, one a little younger."

For a few seconds we stared at each other right in the eye. He had one thumb hooked in a pocket and he was other holding his groceries with the other hand. All I could manage to do was stand there, cupping my grapefruits. It'd be easy to say it was chemistry, like we had made a connection, but I think I know what it really was. He was thinking of how things could've been with us, in a perfect world. Then he was thinking of the way things probably would be, in the real world. Anyway, that's what I was thinking. If he was thinking the same thing then maybe that was chemistry. I don't know.

He said, "Well, take care. Of your girl and yourself."

As he turned to go, I said, "Wait. Hang on. I mean, start over. Can we? I don't know." I juggled around the grapefruits and my purse so I could stick out my hand, and then I said, "My name's Rayanne. Most people call me Rudy. That's Whitney. She never does anything I tell her to."

He had a real good, easy smile. He took my hand and squeezed it. Strong, hard, but warm, and he knew the right way to shake hands with a lady.

I asked him, "You live around here? Wanna get a beer sometime?"

"No," he said. "I live in Las Cruces. I'm just passing through."

"Oh," I said. "Okay."

Then he said, "But I'll be passing back through in a week, going the other way."

"Oh," I said. "Okay."

He said, "It's real good to meet you, Rudy."

I said, "Mm. You, too. Didn't catch your name, though."

"Well, some folks call me Mr. Cool Ranch. But you can call me Ricky."

WAITING FOR DONNA

Donna's waiting for me on the porch when I pull up. She gets in the car but doesn't say hi. She just sits there. So, I sit there. We sit there in the driveway of our house.

I really should pull down that jungle gym. It looks like hell. The paint's all flaked off the wood, and any kid who goes near it is going to get a handful of splinters. It's been ten years since Sara or Taylor played on it. The thing is, I built it out of cedar timbers sunk in concrete about four feet under the ground. I'll need a steam shovel and dynamite to tear it out.

The lawn looks okay, but weeds are coming up between the slabs of the driveway. Donna's got some neighbor kid mowing every week. Wouldn't let me do it.

It's funny. She hasn't told anyone in our family that I've moved out, but she doesn't want the neighbors to think I'm moving back in.

The neighbor kid's not paying attention to the driveway. Or the walkway. Nobody's trimming the trees or shrubs, either. The lilac looks like it's gonna swallow the garage. No one's paying attention to the weeds. No one's paying attention but me.

After a few seconds Donna says, "Well. Can we go?"

I say, "No 'hi'? No 'how are you'?"

She lets out a big sigh. "Hi, Larry. How are you."

It's Thursday. Donna knows I've been golfing on Thursdays. All these years she's been nagging me to "get out and exercise." Now she needs a ride on the day I go golfing.

I say, "You do know what today is, right?"

She says, "I know perfectly well what today is."

I ask her, "So, why today? Why not yesterday or tomorrow?"

She says, "This was the only day they had open."

I tell her, "There's some weed spray in the garage by the lawnmower. Green bottle about yay-big. If you hit those weeds on the driveway every coupla days they'll quit coming up."

"Kay. Can we go?"

"No," I say.

"Larry," she huffs. "Why? What now?"

"You still haven't told me where you're going."

She finally looks over. But she's glaring at me. She looks out the windshield again and says, "Just head into town. I'll show you where it's at."

I tell her, "There's lots of ways to get into town. Is it downtown? Is it out by the Interstate? If it's out by the Interstate, I don't want to go downtown. I'll hit every light on the way through."

She lets out another big sigh. Like I'm the one who's difficult. Like I'm the one who wanted to separate.

"This isn't my fault, Donna. You want to separate? Fine. But if you call me for a ride, at least be civil to me. At least give me decent driving directions."

I don't really say that. Not out loud.

"It's downtown," she says.

"Where at downtown?"

"Across from that Mexican restaurant with the umbrellas out front," she says. "On Broad Street, or Grove."

"Well, which one?"

"Broad. I think. It's a long brick building," she says. "You know, dark red brick. There's only two Mexican places downtown, Larry, and one of them's a Taco Bell."

I say, "Okay, I know the place. It's not on Broad." I back out of the driveway. "It's where the eye doctor used to be, where Taylor got his contacts. Before that it was a vet clinic for a while. We took Mi Mi there when she was a puppy."

"Okay," she says. "So."

"So, just say we're going to the old vet clinic. Or the old eye doctor. In fact, when we first moved here it was the DMV. That's all you had to say—the old DMV. You don't remember taking Mi Mi to get her shots when she was just little?"

Apparently, she doesn't.

We head downtown. But I can't put my arm on the middle thing between the seats. Donna doesn't tell me not to, but whenever I do she moves her arm and leans away a little to make sure I don't touch her. So now I don't know what to do with my arm. All these years I've been driving around with my arm on the middle thing in between the seats. Now it's like I've got an extra arm in the car with me and I don't know where to put it.

I ask her, "What's the matter with your car?"

Technically, it's not her car. It's mine. They're both

mine. Both cars are in my name. But I don't say that. Can you imagine if I did?

Donna says, "Sara's got it. She went to the lake with a friend."

"You let her take the Subaru out there? That road? The way she drives?"

Donna says, "She's not a kid."

"That's my point. She needs to be out on her own. Get her degree, get her own car."

We hit every stoplight. The car stops and goes. I don't know where to put my arm. Donna just sits there.

I ask her, "What's this place we're going to? What is it this time?"

She says, "I don't know."

This was a big part of her problem. She never knew anything. She'd shut down. Always depressed about something. She get diagnosed with some new thing. Her bladder, her intestines, and that would make her depressed.

I'd always say, "Donna, tell me what's the matter. Tell me what I can do."

And she would say, "I don't know," but she knew.

I ask her, "What, you don't know where I'm taking you?"

She says, "I don't know what they call it. It's a lot of little medical offices."

"So, another therapist," I say. "Another shrink, psychologist, healer."

I look over at her. She's got her feet on the seat, knees up by her chin. That's how she sits when she gets this way. All balled up.

"What's wrong this time?" I ask.

She glares at me. Like I'm the one.

"Larry," she says, "I don't know what's wrong. That's

why I go."

I pull up to the building. It's where we brought Taylor when he was thirteen, fourteen. Didn't want to wear glasses anymore. He was on the basketball team and trying to get a girlfriend. I did the same thing when I was chasing girls. I'd shove my glasses in my pocket and squint all night. First time I went out with Donna I couldn't even tell what she looked like.

I ask her, "You don't remember coming here with Taylor? He was so excited he didn't have to wear those glasses anymore. Remember? Then he got acne."

Donna says, "I gotta go in. Can you wait here? It'll be about an hour. I can call someone if you can't."

"Well if you can call someone else to take you home, why didn't you call them to pick you up in the first place and leave me out of it? Coulda been golfing right now."

I don't really say that.

"Yeah, I'll wait."

She goes inside. I get out and lean on the car. It's nice out. Pretty soon I see Chris Hutchins walking past. He used to do our taxes. Must've moved his office downtown.

He says, "How's it going, Larry?"

I smile, wave. "Just waiting for my wife."

That's not really what he asked, but he nods. I don't know if Chris knows about me and Donna. I don't know who knows and who doesn't, so I've decided to act like everything's okay and nobody knows. It's working so far. Besides, I just wanted to say it that way. And it's true. I am waiting for my wife. Makes it feel like all the other times I waited for her. Like it's just a normal day, running errands, waiting for Donna.

"You got an office down here now?" I ask him.

I could give a shit where is office is, but I ask him that because I know he'll start talking to me about doing mine and Donna's taxes again sometime, and I can pretend to listen, and if I pretend hard enough, he'll still be here when Donna comes back, so then if he maybe knows something but not everything about Donna and me, he can at least tell the people who know us that he saw us driving around together.

Chris starts talking. I start pretending.

And it works. Donna finally comes back out. Chris says hi to her and then gives me his card and says he's gotta get going but that we should call him.

"We will," I tell him. "We will. So long, Chris."

"What was that about?" Donna asks me. "He thinks he's still doing our taxes?"

"Just being friendly," I say.

It was a lot more than an hour, by the way, not that I'm keeping track, not that I tell her it was longer than an hour. Donna's got a bunch of papers with her. She's sorting through them. We get in the car. She reads the papers.

"You ever think if you quit going to all these therapists and started talking to the actual people in your life, you might start feeling better?"

I really say this.

At first, Donna just sits there. Doesn't even look up from her papers. I think I know what she wants to say, and I can tell she's not going to say it. She opens her mouth to say it but stops herself and then her mouth shuts. Doesn't matter. I know what it was gonna be. Basically.

But then shakes her head a little, and now I can tell she's going to say the thing she was going to but didn't. She looks up from the papers, takes a big breath, and says, "There are things I need to put behind me."

That's not what I thought she was gonna say.

But I tell her what I was going to say back if she'd said the thing I thought she was going to say, because it still fits: "That's your problem. You only remember the things you want to, and the things you want to remember are the bad things. You never remember any of the good things."

I hit every light on the way out of town. Donna goes back to her papers. I got my arm laying in my lap like it's busted.

As I pull into the driveway, she says, "Can I call you next week if I need a ride again?"

"What about the Subaru? What about Sara?"

"Larry," she says, "I'm not saying I will call you. I'm asking if I can. You always ask me what you can do. This is something you can do. So. Can I call you."

"Sure," I say. "Course you can. Just do me a favor and try not to pick the same day again."

"Same day?" she says. She wrinkles her brow, looks over at me. "How could I pick the same day? I'm talking about next week, not next year."

I say, "What are you talking about?"

She says, "What are you talking about?"

I tell her, "I'm talking about Thursdays. I golf on Thursdays now. You've been telling me all this time to get out and exercise. Well, I am. And I feel great. Down eight pounds. So. Just pick some other day next week, that's all. What'd you think I meant?"

She laughs. First she just chuckles, but then she really starts going for it. She's got her forehead in her hand and she laughs and laughs. Not loud, but hard, and it shakes the car a little. Almost gets me laughing, you know, like you do when someone's laughing even if you don't know what it's about. But something tells me not to. Something tells me she's not laughing at something funny.

So, I say, "Mind telling me what's so funny?"

I have no idea what she's about to say.

"Larry. Today's our anniversary."

"Anniversary."

"Yeah," she says. "Our wedding anniversary."

I say, "I'll be damned."

She says, "Yeah."

"I'll be damned." It's all I can think of to say.

WHY I WON'T GO TO THE MOVIES
WITH BRIAN SNOW

He's got lousy taste in movies, for one thing. If it's not an action movie, he'll classify it as a "chick flick" or "hipster porn." Or he'll say, "Ah, that's just one of those movies that we all know is a buncha bullshit, but pretentious college people watch it and they're all too scared to admit it's boring."

He talks constantly, for another thing. That's one of the big reasons. I mean he never stops. During the movie, I'm saying. Talks so much I'd actually be surprised if the guy has ever seen an entire movie.

I asked him one time, I said, "Hey, you know the part in 'Apocalypse Now' when the dude slaughters the water buffalo?"

He said, "What? No. When's that?"

Can you believe that? Who doesn't remember the part in "Apocalypse Now" when the dude slaughters the water buffalo?

And he'll never go anywhere with you—it's always got to be you going with him, it has to be his thing. When you ask him to go somewhere or do something, he's always going ice climbing or kayaking. Most people just say, "No, I can't tonight—I'm heading home to get some sleep," or "No, I need to reinstall Windows on my computer," but Snow's always getting ready to take off somewhere to do some exotic combination of things, like backpacking somewhere to go base jumping.

What kind of person insists on being called by his last name, anyway? I know everyone calls him Snow, but that's because he tells you to, and he enforces it like a rule. Try calling him Brian one time. He'll let you know.

He works at the magazine where I work. That's how I met him. He works in Circulation—he's not a writer. A couple weeks later, he pulls into my driveway one night around 6 o'clock and honks his horn. He doesn't even get out of his truck. Just honks until I come out. I'm in a t-shirt and dirty sweatpants. I was getting ready to eat something and then sack out.

He rolls down his window and goes, "Hey."

I say, "Hey. What's up? Something wrong at work?"

He says, "No, I'm going to the movies. You in?"

That's how it starts. He pulls up and honks and you're either in or out. No call. No text. So, I ask him what he's going to see. It's a World War II movie.

He says, "Come on. Are you in?"

See, this is the kind of guy I am. I wasn't going to do anything that night. I was getting ready to eat something and sack out. Cynthia had called me earlier wanting to watch the Rangers game together, and I actually turned her down because I was tired. And I knew she'd be pissed, but I really was exhausted. But this is the kind of guy I am—Snow's the new guy, I want to be nice, so I say, "Okay. Fine. I'm in."

I turn to go back into the house and he says, "Hold

up. Where you going?"

I tell him, "I'm gonna change clothes."

He says, "What for? It's a movie. It'll be dark."

I say, "Can I at least get my wallet?"

He says I don't need any money because he's got free tickets from the magazine. He says, "Hurry up. Get in. It's starting."

So, I'm wearing sweats. I've got no money. Even left a ham and cheese Hot Pocket in the microwave. Meanwhile, we're flying down the street in the opposite direction of the theater.

I say, "Where we going?"

He says, "I gotta stop and get something to eat."

I say, "I thought the movie was starting."

He says, "We'll be fine."

We get to the place and there's fifteen cars in the drive-through, so Snow parks and then goes right up to the register and cuts in front of about five people.

Guy behind us says, "Hey, you can't jump in line like that."

Snow says, "Sorry man, we're in a big hurry."

I tell him, I say, "Hey, Snow, we can't cut in front of all these people."

He says, "We'll be fine."

Meanwhile, the guy behind us is telling his wife, "I'm getting ready to kick these guys' asses. As soon as I'm done eating, I swear I'm gonna kick their asses."

But Snow's already in the middle of his order. He says, "I need a double cheeseburger with plenty of ketchup."

This high school girl is taking the order. She says, "Sorry, did you say no ketchup?"

He says, "No, I said plenty of ketchup."

She says, "So, you want extra ketchup?"

He says, "No, I want the right amount of ketchup." He says, "Sometimes your cheeseburgers don't have enough ketchup to cover the patty. Just make sure you give me the right amount of ketchup, enough to cover the meat."

She blinks a few times and says, "I'm not the one that's going to make it."

So he says, "Make a note, then. Tell the guy to put plenty of ketchup on it."

She blinks again and says, "I can't really make a note about that. The orders are on a computer. Back there."

Meanwhile, the people behind us are super pissed, and they're getting organized, like those people on the plane on 9/11. They're making plans.

Snow tells the girl, "Then go back there and tell him. It's like fifteen feet. Is it that guy right there? I'll tell him myself. Hey. You. Burger maker. We need plenty of ketchup on this next one."

I ask Snow if he can cover me if I order something. I tell him I'm starving.

He says, "Mmm, sorry dude, all I have is a twenty. If I get you something I won't be able to get any popcorn. Know what? I'll share my popcorn with you. You'll be fine."

But he doesn't get any popcorn. We run out of the burger place and when we get to the theater, the movie has already started, so we run straight in. It's at least halfway over. You can always tell when a World War II movie is halfway over because the Germans look really ragged and skinny. The Germans in this movie look like they're about to keel over from starvation.

And so am I. But Snow doesn't care. And he's still eating the cheeseburger. Right in front of me.

He says, "This is what I always tell people. If you

want your burger done right. Like if you think they don't cook it right or they don't put the right amount of ketchup on, you've got to take matters in your own hands."

Then he tells me about this delicacy he had when he went sport-climbing in Vietnam. We're right in the middle of the movie and he starts telling me about his trip to Vietnam.

He says, "Only a few people in the whole country even know the recipe, and you used to have to get permission from the government to even cook it. Think about that—government permission just to make a recipe. They used to make it for the highest-up leaders in the world. Like Kissinger and George Bush. Their pictures were on the wall. They ate this government recipe at that restaurant. Colin Powell and the Clintons. Anyway, they take these baby ducks, like just hatched, and they feed 'em to these huge carp. Carp eats like five or six baby ducks and starts digesting them. After about twelve hours they take the carp outta the water and throw it into a huge pot of wine, guts and all, and boil it for hours. Then they cut open the carp's belly and take out the baby ducks. They're all soft by this time, and you eat 'em whole, bones and feet and bills and everything. They're soft like Vienna sausages. And do you know what they dip them in?"

I shake my head. I really want to know.

"Ketchup. No lie. They discovered it while our guys were over there fighting the war. American ketchup."

Then he stops talking. For effect, I think. I think he wants to let it sink in or something. I look up at the movie. It's clearly almost over. Nobody's even fighting anymore. They don't care. Just a bunch of guys playing poker down in their foxhole.

Snow says, "Did you see that? Those look like modern-day dollar bills. Did dollar bills look like that back then?"

By now I'm just sick to death of him. I'm trying to shut him up. For my sake. For everyone else in the theater. I think maybe if he shuts up, the war will start up again. I say, "I'm not sure. Maybe. I don't know. Just watch."

He says, "I know they changed 'em right after the war. When did the war get over? Nineteen forty?"

"World War II?" I say. "No. Forty-five."

He says, "Forty-five? Then when did the Vietnam War get over? The fifties?

"No," I say. "Seventies. Mid-seventies. You're thinking of Korea."

He says, "No way. Nam was over by nineteen sixty, tops."

See, this is the kind of guy I am. I want to help him. I want to explain to him that the United States dropped nuclear bombs on Japan in August 1945 and the Japanese couldn't give up quick enough after that. They signed the papers in September and then things got kind of chilly with the commies in the fifties, which is how we got involved in Korea. And Vietnam, for that matter, when Eisenhower sent advisors over there to help the French, who'd been there since the 1880s. After that, we had troops in Vietnam till the North broke through in seventy-five. That's the kind of guy I am—I'm trying to help. Problem is, people are turning around and yelling at us now.

Guy in front of me turns around and says, "Hey. Asshole. Shut up."

Snow asks him, "Hey, do you know when World War II ended?"

Guy says, "No! Shut up!"

Snow points at the movie screen and says, "We're talking about World War II, jerk." He turns to me and says, "Can you believe this asshole? Shushing me for talking about World War II *in a movie* about World War II."

I try to tell him, "World War II was over in forty-five. Vietnam was over in seventy-five. Now shush."

He shakes his head, thinks I'm just guessing, but I know these things. I read books. He can't even remember the part in "Apocalypse Now" where the dude slaughters the water buffalo. He shakes his head—like I'm the idiot.

Finally, the movie gets over. I have no idea who even won. For all I know, the Germans won that time. I'm just happy to get out of there because I'm so hungry I'm getting ready to collapse. I still hate that movie.

We get back on the road and he's flying across town again, so I ask him where we're going and he says he wants to stop by Spooky's. Says he wants to get a beer and see if the game is over because he doesn't have cable yet.

I say, "I can't go into Spooky's looking like this."

He says, "You'll be fine."

I think, okay, I can at least eat a couple bowls of peanuts, and then this'll all be over and he pulls up and honks again, I won't even go outside. So we get to Spooky's and guess who's there? Cynthia. She's sitting there with all her girl friends.

She says, "Hey, James. Thought you said you were tired."

I can barely look her in the face. I know she's looking at my dirty sweatpants, so I try to change the subject by introducing her to Snow.

I say, "Cynthia, this is Brian Snow. He works at the magazine now. In Circulation."

Can you believe that? I introduced my girlfriend to Brian Snow.

Of course he says, "Call me Snow." Then—get this—he says to her, "This guy bailed on you to go to the movies with me?" He turns to me and says, "Are you nuts? You picked that movie over her? That movie sucked. They were using modern-day dollar bills and everything."

Cynthia gives me a look, but she laughs it off. I'll hear about it later, but right now she's being nice to both of us. I try to get between her and Snow but by this time he's all over her. He squeezes into the booth. There's no room for me. He starts telling her and her friends about how he just got back from building schools in South America.

"You want to learn to surf?" he asks Cynthia. "Go to Peru and build a school. The workers'll take you surfing every weekend."

I say, "Hey, Snow, why don't you grab us a beer?"

Cynthia gives me the look and says, "James, that's rude. Snow's the new guy. Why don't you get us one?"

Snow says, "Yeah, James, *you* grab *me* a beer."

He reaches in his pocket and I think, finally, he'll at least spring for the beer. But he gets out his car keys instead. He throws them to me. It's like one of those big key wads with a car remote and a memory stick and about eleven key chains from different places.

"If you're buying," he says, "I guess I won't be driving."

The biggest key chain is a unicorn made out of pink foam. Says *DENMARK* on it. I hold up the unicorn, like I can't possibly be expected to carry it around.

Snow says, "You like that? My sister gave it to me. Don't lose it."

What could I do? I turn around and walk away. I go to the bar, watch the Rangers awhile. They're down by two. Bartender asks me what I want. I tell him I don't even have my wallet on me because I went to the movies with this guy who got free tickets from the magazine where we work, and then he wanted to come by and see how the Rangers were doing because he doesn't have cable yet. But the bartender doesn't want to hear any of that. Plus my sweat pants don't have any pockets, so I'm holding this big wad of keys with a foam unicorn. I eat a bowl of pretzels someone left behind. They're stale. The Rangers are getting creamed.

When I go back to the booth to tell them all I don't have any money, Cynthia is laughing her head off.

"No, I swear to god," says Snow. "Every grocery store in Peru, every taxi cab, everywhere you go, you hear Depeche Mode."

Everyone laughs. Snow is standing up on the seat of the booth and pantomiming some kind of Peruvian surfing maneuver and singing "People are People." Cynthia gives him this flirty little slug on the arm, just like she did when we were first going out. I stand there with Snow's Danish unicorn. I'm thinking, it's only about twenty blocks to my house, and I get ready to tell Snow I'm taking off.

But then Cynthia looks over at me as Snow launches into the story about the baby ducks and the carp and Richard Nixon. She's pretending to pay attention to him but she's looking at me. I shrug at her. She smiles and shakes her head and kind of rolls her eyes and then touches her hair and looks away, and it's this like very complicated series of gestures, but I know exactly what it means. She's saying: "I get it. I think I know what happened, and I'm not mad, but you can tell me later." Cynthia gets it, and I get that she gets it, and she gets that, too. And just like that, we're good.

Snow sees me. He looks right at me but he says to Cynthia: "Hey. Cynthia. You're smart. You'll know this one. When did the Vietnam War get over?" Then he looks at her.

She says, "Oh, I have no idea. Wasn't it like mid-seventies?"

You know what Snow says? Want to know what that prick says to me?

He turns to me, says, "See? I told you."

THE SKIN OF MISERY

If you were in the Dramatic Performance Program, I wouldn't have to tell you who Julian LeMarc is. I wouldn't have to tell you anything about him. In the Program, everyone knows Julian LeMarc, and in the Program, everyone knows he's a badass. He weighs maybe a hundred and twenty pounds, short and skinny, and he dresses real gay, but he is what he is: a hotshot New York City director.

I don't know how they feel about him back there, but out here? He scares the living shit out of everybody. That's the first thing you need to know about Julian LeMarc.

The second thing is, we all love him.

We absolutely worship him. He does plays in New York and Paris and everywhere. Knows everything. He comes to the university for three weeks every fall and does an intensive seminar on stage directing. The department saves up for a year to pay him. It's impossible to get into. There's a waiting list every single fall. You kind of have to know someone who knows someone who can get you in.

Of course, I didn't know anyone who knew anyone at all, so there was no way I could get in. But, get this, I got in anyway—not as a student, but as an actor. See, every student in the seminar directs a whole scene, so every students needs a couple-three actors. They pick a scene or write one, then they cast it, rehearse it, direct it, the whole deal. LeMarc watches the scenes, gives everyone feedback, gives everyone a grade, and so on. But he also picks the best scene of the seminar, and the winner gets an internship with LeMarc back in NYC, and then they come back to campus and co-direct a play together. It's like this amazing opportunity. Even the intern plays are hard to get tickets to.

And that's basically what you need to know about LeMarc.

Somehow, my friend Dimitri got into the seminar. I don't know how. He's not what you would call really bright or really good in school. He definitely must have known someone who knew someone. But after he got into the seminar, his girlfriend Tisha asked me to go with him and be in his scene. And it sounded really good. I mean to just get into that seminar and hear what LeMarc had to say would be really great. Doing a little acting would be even better. But I didn't have the time that semester. I told her—"I don't have time."

She said, "Brandon, you have to. You know what's going to happen. You know how Dimitri is. He needs actors, but what he really needs is someone to watch out for him. You know what I'm talking about. If you're there, you can watch out for him. Please? Help me out."

It's really hard to say no to Tisha. And I did know what she was talking about. So, she didn't have to twist my arm. She said she and Dimitri would cook for me all fall semester, so I could do homework, said Dimitri would drive me to classes so I wouldn't have to spend so much time on the bus. She said they'd make it worth my time.

"Okay, Tish," I said. "Yeah. I'll do it."

Dimitri even gave me the lead role in his scene. That felt good, too. And it wasn't super likely, but if Dimitri's scene somehow got picked by LeMarc, he told me he'd put me in his internship play, and I'd get to work directly with LeMarc. But hell, even if Dimitri didn't win, I could at least pick up some technique, some craft. And I didn't get any credits for it, but it was free, so, it really started looking like a win-win for me.

So I get to the theater on the first day of the seminar and the whole class is scared shitless. The students, I mean. They're terrified. I'm not kidding. They're sitting in the seats of the theater, and all us actors are up on the stage looking down at them. I see their faces; they're petrified. White knuckles on the armrests, eyes darting around like they're in seriously deep trouble. LeMarc isn't even there yet and they're truly bugging out, knees bouncing. Like a bunch of little kids at the dentist's office.

There's one more thing you need to know about LeMarc.

Every year during his seminar, something really bad happens. LeMarc loses his shit and eats somebody alive. Every year, he destroys some poor student. It's like the school has to give up one student every year for the privilege of having him teach. Like a sacrifice to a god.

Dimitri said one year LeMarc told some girl that she was wasting his time, everybody's time, that she had no business taking his seminar. He called her a hack, called her a wannabe, booted her outta the class. It was the third day, in front of everyone. She ran out the door, dropped out of school, and moved home. The university didn't do anything about it. Dimitri said no one ever saw her again.

Another time, LeMarc got into a fistfight with a student. Apparently, he told the kid, "You just might be good enough someday to manage a shift of strung-out waitresses at the Denny's by the freeway off-ramp, but you're never gonna direct actors, sweetie. It's just never gonna happen."

The kid punched LeMarc in the jaw. LeMarc called the cops, laughed at the kid as they hauled him off. The university kicked the poor guy out of school and pressed charges.

"Lemme guess," I said to Dimitri. "No one ever saw him again either?"

"No," said Dimitri, "he is literally working at a Denny's now. He is literally managing strung-out waitresses. That is what I've heard."

Dimitri said something like this happens every year. They call it "getting LeMarc'ed."

When LeMarc first came into the theater, I couldn't believe anyone could ever be scared of him. He's so small and swishy. Bald head, little square glasses. But I had to admit really quick that I was glad I wasn't actually in the seminar. It got intense almost instantly. He walked up and down the aisles, yelling at the students, right in their faces sometimes, like an army sergeant, a gay little army sergeant. You wouldn't think a little guy like that could yell so loud. You wouldn't think someone with a femmy voice like that could be so, I don't know, like, *dominant*. But he'd go, "Listen up!" and the whole room would flinch at the same time. Even me.

And on top of all this, remember that everyone wants to be the best in the class, too. Everyone wants their own scene to win, so they're showing off, talking big. They're asking for it; they have to. Every time LeMarc asks a question, every single one of them raises their hands, like in kindergarten—"pick me! pick me!"

Everyone except Dimitri.

Tisha was right; he was totally in over his head. He's joking with the girl next to him, laughing. That's how he is. Nothing ever bothers him, nothing ever gets to him, which in one way is kind of a good thing, but he never pays attention either, so he's always getting himself into trouble. Like when he got stuck in that giant snowstorm out on the state highway over Christmas break. Didn't even have a coat with him. He called Tisha on his cell phone, but the call kept dropping and then his phone died. She didn't know where he was, what was going on. No one did. Highway Patrol finally brought him home about seven the next morning, but all that night we were saying, "Where's Dimitri? Did he make it home? Has anyone heard?"

Truthfully, I have no idea why Dimitri even wanted to be in LeMarc's seminar. Don't get me wrong. Dimitri's a great guy, and funny as hell, but you've got to be organized to direct a play. And ambitious and assertive. You've got to be able to take charge. Dimitri? He's not even listening. He's talking to the girl; he's on his phone.

This goes on for a few days—the yelling, the lecturing. LeMarc asks questions. Everyone has a guess. Everyone's wrong. More yelling.

He says, "What is the director's most important tool?"

Every hand goes up.

Then he says, "What's the director's most important tool, and please answer only if you can do so without making yourself sound even stupider than you actually are."

Half the hands go down.

He points at a girl and says, "You, in the beret, put your hand down for the rest of this day. I haven't even finished my coffee yet and I'm sick to death of you. You, in the turtleneck, answer the question, but if you try to bring up that shitty little Shakespearean festival thing you were in again, so help me god: I—will—fail you."

The actors are up on the stage watching all of this, like some kind of turned-around play. We're betting on who's gonna get screamed at next, who's gonna get LeMarc'ed. LeMarc walks up and down the theater with his clipboard. We're waiting for him to just smack somebody with it. Not one single one of us would be surprised if he did. The students show up earlier and earlier so they don't have to sit in the aisle seats.

Finally, we start performing. The actors got the scenes a couple weeks in advance. We've been reading together forever when the seminar begins, so we've got the lines down. Some of us have even started blocking and thinking about costumes. We sure as hell don't want LeMarc to yell at us, but as the strain really starts to wear the students down, the actors are pretty like what you would call chilled out. Smug, really.

Dimitri's scene is from a play called "The Skin of Misery." Some Czechoslovakian playwright. Very heavy. Very dense. Probably the most emotionally loaded part I've ever played. Last summer I was Jerry in "Clash By Night" at a dinner theater in the city, and that didn't come close to this.

I have no idea why Dimitri picked that play. It's the complete opposite of his personality. I was thinking, keep it simple, man. Keep it real. Let's do some Mamet, you know, Tennessee Williams. "Speed-the-Plow," or hell even "The Hairy Ape." But we were gonna make this thing of Dimitri's work, too—the actors, I mean. We'd made up our minds. We were gonna rattle the boards, chew on the set.

There's two of us in the scene: me and this girl, Sabrianna. There's another guy in the scene, but he has three or four lines at the very start and then he exits. His name is Randall. Kind of a loser. Mostly it's me and Sabrianna. I have way more lines and one really good speech. Sabrianna's got some good lines, too, but she's there for all the wrong reasons. And if you think I'm just saying that because she wouldn't sleep with me, I'm not. Yeah, I was laughing my ass off with everyone else when LeMarc was giving them the business, but I was truly serious about our scene. I'm a professional. Sabrianna's basically in the program because her parents pay her tuition and classes in the Program are easy. It's obvious that's why she's there. But me, I want to act professionally—for me, the classes aren't easy.

So, we're doing our scene and really nailing it. Even Sabrianna is landing on every line like a goddess, but Dimitri keeps stopping us, starting us over. Pretty soon everyone's worn out. Dimitri rubs his eyes, looking like he can barely keep awake. Maintaining the intensity of the scene, the emotion—it's exhausting, especially for me. Because I'm all over the stage, waving my arms and yelling, so it's physically demanding, too. Plus I want our scene to win more than anyone, including probably Dimitri, so I'm giving it everything I've got, but I can tell that LeMarc is getting ready to blow his stack. He's right on the edge and Dimitri doesn't even see it. Even I'm starting to get scared. Sabrianna and I are looking at each other like, "It's Dimitri. Dimitri's the one who gets LeMarc'ed."

I make my entrance for about the eighth time. I come in through this door. It's just a doorframe with a door, and I bust through it to make my entrance. I say to Sabrianna, "You know what I was looking for, don'tcha? You know I only wanted someone to be there for me, someone to wait with me, but you couldn't, couldja? Couldn't even wait an hour."

Then Sabrianna has a line, but Dimitri isn't even watching us.

LeMarc jumps up and goes, "Stop stop stop stop stop."

I know this is it. This is where Dimitri gets LeMarc'ed. This is where Dimitri gets kicked out of the class, hauled off to jail, drops out of school, and moves back home. This is the last time anybody sees Dimitri. And I feel this weird sort of tragic energy building in the room, because I was supposed to be there for Dimitri, but the class wasn't really set up in a way that I could ever defend Dimitri against LeMarc, so it was kind of a doomed mission to begin with. I think about Tish. Sabrianna and I stand on the stage. We watch LeMarc watching Dimitri.

Then LeMarc gets up from his seat in the theater, goes into the aisle, walks over to Dimitri, and crouches in front of him. He stares Dimitri in the eye for the longest time.

He says, "Dimitri, I know this is hard for you. Because you're not very smart, are you? Someone told me you're not, and I believed it right away. I'm thinking you won't be offended by that because you know it, too, that you're not a smart guy. That's not your role, is it? That's not your part. But I know you're creative, Dimitri, and I know you're sensitive, and I know you can read the energy around here. So, don't let's use your brain right now. Turn it off. Let's give that tiny little instrument a break. I want you to use your heart. Right now, I want you to *feel*, not think. Can you do that for me?"

Dimitri nods, slowly.

LeMarc says, "Kay. Feel the answer for me, Dimitri. What is the weak link here? In your scene, of all the things that can go wrong—the set, the actors, the lines, even you, the director—what would you say is the weakest link in your production?"

Dimitri looks around, looks down at his notes. It's the storm on the state highway all over again. He's got no gas, no coat, no phone. I'm thinking, damn you, Dimitri. You could have won this.

LeMarc takes a deep breath, and he lets it out right in Dimitri's face. He says, "Let me put it another way, so that even you can understand: *who* in this scene is your weakest link?"

Dimitri immediately says, "Is it—me?"

LeMarc shakes his head. Real slow. Says, "Guess again."

I'm thinking, oh, I get it—he means Sabrianna. Because Randall's a complete loser but he's actually doing just fine and he's off stage at this point, so it can't really be him, and how can there be something wrong with the set? There's a door and a chair. There is no set.

Then I think, wait a second. Sabrianna's really only got a couple good lines, and, honestly, she's doing good. It can't be her. So, it's not Sabrianna, and it's not

Randall, and it's not Dimitri.

Dimitri bows his head and says, "It's Brandon."

And LeMarc stands up and says, "Yes! Yes yes yes. You knew it from the start, didn't you? It *is* Brandon. Brandon *is* the weak link." He turns to the rest of the class and yells, "Everyone get that?"

They're already nodding. They knew, too. Every head in the theater, nodding.

Then LeMarc looks at me. "Brandon? Got that?"

I nod.

LeMarc turns back to Dimitri, says, "What are you going to do, Dimitri? He may be a shit actor, but he's your shit actor. You're the director. This is your problem. What are you going to do?"

Dimitri looks at his notes again, but LeMarc rips them away and throws them across the theater. They go really far.

LeMarc stands there for a few seconds and says, "Dimitri, I like you. And so I want you to watch me. Pay attention."

LeMarc hops up onto the stage. The whole place goes silent.

He walks up to me, real close, and says, "Brandon, who are you?"

Obviously, he's trying to set me up. He thinks I'm going to say Brandon, but I say, "Reza." That's my character's name. I say, "I'm Reza."

He says, "Wrong! Who are you?"

Now I know it's a trap, so I say, "Brandon?"

"Wrong! Who—are—you."

Now I'm panicking. I say, "I don't know."

He shouts, "Exactly!" He roars it. "Exactly! You do not know who you are. Nobody knows who you are! If you were doing your job, I wouldn't have to ask you. I wouldn't have to fly all the way out here to this shitty little town, make poor dumb Dimitri feel awful, come up here on the stage, and ask you who you are to your face. *You're* supposed to show *me*, Brandon. You're supposed to show all of us. You understand me?

I nod again.

"Good. Good. So. Show me who you are. Show us all."

"Okay." That's all I can say.

Lemarc looks at me over the top of his glasses. It would sound corny if I said he looked right through me, but that's exactly what happened. He has these brown eyes that look kind of like flames around the pupil. Like flames and two tiny black holes. He's staring at me and it feels like he just downloads my whole personality, my whole soul, right in that second.

He says, "You have no idea what I'm talking about, do you."

It's not really a question, so I don't answer.

He runs his tongue over his lips. Then he steps away from and looks me up and down, like he's sizing me up for a new suit. He says, "All right. Take off your shoes."

I look at him like I maybe didn't hear him right.

He says, "Your shoes. Take 'em off. Come on, come on."

I take them off, but believe me, I don't want to because sometimes my feet smell. Sometimes I have a foot odor problem, but I do what he says. I take off my shoes, take off my socks.

Then he says, "Take off your shirt."

I take it off.

He looks at me some more, says, "You know what? The pants, too. Off. Take 'em off. Go ahead."

I didn't want to, I really didn't. My underwear is gray

and sort of see-through in the back because it's worn out. It's embarrassing. My legs are white. My whole body's white. I'm flabby.

But there's one more final critical thing you need to know about LeMarc.

Every year, someone gets royally nuked, yes. Every seminar, every year. Someone gets LeMarc'ed, wiped off the map, disappeared, and that's the price the school pays.

But every year, there's also a breakthrough.

Someone in the seminar always has this giant epiphany or mind-altering experience, and after that they sort of rise to a new level. Like LeMarc brings them up to his plane of existence. And as much as they talk about whoever gets LeMarc'ed, the breakthroughs are what everyone really remembers.

Like Miranda Dobson—took LeMarc's seminar, got the internship, and now she's a bigshot in Chicago. Or that kid Trent Gleason. If you were in the Program, you'd know his name, too. He took LeMarc's seminar and won with a scene from "Long Day's Journey." When they performed the whole play on campus, the dean cried. He wept. He had tears dripping all down his face. That must have been three years ago and people still talk about it.

I could've said no. Even Julian LeMarc can't make a university student get undressed. Not these days. But it feels like this is just an extension of the scene, or that LeMarc and I are playing a new scene, just us two, for the whole class. Am I getting LeMarc'ed? Maybe. But every eye is on me. Everyone's watching. I can feel that attention that real actors talk about, that bio-feedback—how it's so quiet, how you can't hear a cough or the slightest shifting in the seats. I can feel every single pair of eyeballs watching.

So I go for the breakthrough. Dimitri let us down. Or he let us down at least as much as I did. LeMarc said so himself—Dimitri's the director, it's Dimitri's problem. But I'll make this breakthrough happen for me and for all of us. Because I'm a professional. I'm ready. So I take it all off and stand there in my see-through underwear and pale flabby skin.

LeMarc starts real quiet and gets louder and louder. He says, "Brandon, I want you to forget everything. You're playing this angry, and you're playing it big, but this isn't about being big or angry. It's about telling us who you are. It's about honesty. I want you to forget the character, forget the anger, forget Dimitri. Forget all of it! All I want you to remember are the lines."

He waves me away and goes and sits down, and the theater erupts in applause.

"Forget everything," says LeMarc when they stop clapping. "Come in that door, and show us who you are." He's sitting in his chair now, yelling at me: "Show us, Brandon. Show us."

So I did. I forgot it all. I put everything out of my mind except my lines. I got to the other side of that door, and I felt it. Without my clothes, standing on the other side of that free-standing door, I knew who I was. I knew I could be Brandon and Reza. I could show the audience Reza's betrayal, and the playwright's betrayal, but it would be the story of my betrayal, too. I could tell the story of all three of us, like the Holy Trinity—the playwright in Reza, Reza in me, me embodying all three, speaking with one voice, showing everyone who I was and telling them a little about who they were, too.

I burst through the door; I practically knock it down.

Sabrianna jumps back, but I grab her, take her in my arms. We never rehearsed it that way, but I do it anyway. I grab her hard.

"You know what I was looking for, don'tcha?" I'm talking right into her mouth. "You know I only wanted someone to be there for me, someone to wait with me, but you couldn't do it, couldja? Couldn't even wait an hour."

Sabrianna's eyes are popped open. She can't even say her line. Nobody says anything for a long time. Everything's quiet.

LeMarc stands up, and then he says, "Well, Dimitri, that's just one thing you can try."

THE PALLBEARERS

We all come together at the church around nine in the morning, and when I say "all," I mean all of us. My mom, my sister Ruth, all five of my brothers.

We're all assembled. Val and his kids have flown in from Vancouver, and Bill's up from Texas. Larry, Ruth, and I drove in from Boise, and Dutch came from Rexburg with his family. Even my brother Ricky's in attendance, despite the fact that six months ago he explicitly swore to me that he wouldn't be.

"When he passes," I told Ricky, "you'll want to pay your respects."

"James," he said, "I ain't got any to pay him."

He came anyway. And I haven't started counting noses yet, but it seems like all Mom and Dad's grandkids are here, too, from all over the place. Dutch and Pat brought their teenage son, Brandon, and their two older sons are here on furlough from fighting in Afghanistan. There are others from all over the country.

Maybe most surprising is Ray, my brother-in-law. He married my sister Deanne back when I was away for college, but then they got into a bad car accident and

Deanne was killed. We still consider him family, but I haven't seen him since Deanne's funeral. In fact, that was probably the last time we were all together this way.

The viewing doesn't start for six hours and there's twenty cars in the parking lot already.

I pull open the front door of the church and Cynthia rushes inside, holding her hair because the wind is blowing like hell. Our kids duck inside under my arm while I keep the door open.

I see Val and Helen and their kids pull into the parking lot in their enormous trucks. They all start climbing out. Val's the oldest; most of his kids are as old as me or older. They're all very tall and thin. Val's into his sixties now and he's starting to show his mileage. His hair is completely white, and he moves slower than I've ever seen. Helen told Cynthia he's having memory problems.

Before I head inside, I pat the front of my suit coat to make sure I've got Dad's letter in the pocket.

In the foyer, Dutch stands with his big arms folded across his big chest. Patricia is sitting on an overstuffed chair behind him, ostensibly awaiting orders but also on standby if Dutch loses his temper. Dutch is third to the oldest, but he was probably first to get to the church, because he always tries to take charge when Dad's not around. I wonder if he knows about the letter.

When he sees us coming in, he points like a traffic cop and says, "Chapel's right through there."

He doesn't know.

"Yeah, Dutch," I answer. "I've been in a church before."

"Don't be a wise ass." His neck is too thick for the top button of his shirt. He adjusts his tie to cover the gap.

Cynthia kisses my cheek and follows the kids into the chapel. It sounds like a new year's party in there. Val and his people come into the foyer behind us. Val has eight kids, all grown, and most of them have kids. They stoop to hug us hello, as if they're of some alien race. The foyer is crammed with people now.

"Chapel's right through there," Dutch keeps repeating, pointing, "and the bathrooms are down this hall on your right."

In a low voice I ask Dutch, "You know why Dad wanted to be buried all the way out here instead of Boise?"

"I assume he wanted to be a pain in the ass. Question is, what do you know about it?"

Okay, so maybe he knows a little. Or he suspects. I shrug at him, but it's too quick, the shrug too big.

He squints his eyes at me for a couple seconds and then says, "Why didn't you shave this morning? It's his funeral. I mean criminy."

Ruth leads Mom in from the parking lot, steadying her by her elbow. Mom blinks at Dutch through her thick eyeglasses.

"Dutch, honey, this isn't our church. Is this the right church?"

"No, Mom, it's not the right church. This is Montana. Didn't anyone tell you?"

"I told her," Ruth insists. She taps her forehead with a finger and mouths, "Not doing well."

"Why don't we just have it at our church?" Mom complains. "Let's have it in Boise, at our church."

"We can't, Mom," says Dutch.

"Why can't we?" she pleads.

Dutch shoots me a glare over the top of her head and says, "Well, that I don't know, Mom."

Bill comes in with his tribe. He's second oldest, and he's nearly as tall as Val, but he's rounder, thicker. So's his wife, Fran. Their kids are chunky and tall, too—Derek and Brian are big as mountains and they're constantly shoving and horseplaying and shouting. Bill's grandkids hit the church like a tidal wave and stream in between the grownups, already in the middle of some kind of full-contact tagging game which also involves tackling.

"What a beautiful drive," says Bill with a sigh. "That sunrise over the hills. What a glorious morning."

Val and Dutch roll their eyes.

Over the noise of the crowd, the funeral director comes into the foyer and introduces himself. His name is Pete Weiss. Pale, skinny guy, no hair. He wants us all in the chapel for a briefing, but wives and kids swarm all around him and down the hallways, checking out the gymnasium, poking around in the kitchen, lining up outside the bathrooms.

Within fifteen minutes, Bill and Val's grandkids find some nursery toys in a sideroom and they start up a game of dodgeball. Pete Weiss tries to break it up, but he takes a direct hit to the lips instead.

"You're out," says Benny, pointing. He's eight. One of Bill's grands.

Pete Weiss checks his mouth for blood and comes to Dutch.

"We can't have kids playing with a ball in here," he says.

Dutch storms into the sideroom and says, "You kids simmer down, hand over the damn ball, and clear the hell out of here."

They follow his instructions—quickly, and in the order they were issued—but Patricia comes up behind

116

Dutch, pokes him in the arm with her thumb, and says, "Dutch, honey, language. Honestly. We're in a church."

Dutch turns to Pete Weiss and says, "Pardon my French, pastor."

"I'm not the pastor," he says. "I'm the funeral director."

"Oh," says Dutch, eyeing the guy like he might be a pretender to that title, too. "Well, never mind then."

Eventually, we shuffle into the chapel. Ray is in there talking with Ricky and the two teen daughters Ricky raised alone when his wife ran off with their insurance man. Dutch patrols the corridors. Mom's irritated, confused. Word is she may have forgotten that Dad is dead. Everyone else is catching up and taking pictures and talking about flights and drive times. Pete Weiss announces he'll be in soon to walk us through the schedule, but he can't seem to get off his phone. No one even pretends to pay attention.

It's a small church house with only one set of lavatories, and after an hour, the ladies' room is clean out of toilet paper. Everyone knows it was Larry's wife Donna and their family. They all have toilet problems—Larry's got a bashful bladder and Donna's got IBS and Crohn's and I don't know what else, but she can't sneeze or laugh or stand up too quick without needing a fresh pair of panties. Both their kids inherited the same problems. Everywhere they go they spend half their time in the toilet.

Donna reports the shortage to Patricia, who reports it to Dutch, who summons Pete Weiss with a wave and a muted horse whistle.

"Pete Weiss," he barks, jabbing his finger at the floor at his feet. "Front and center."

Pete Weiss looks perplexed and indignant but he puts

his hand over his phone and reports to Dutch anyway.

Dutch says, "A gaggle of our ladyfolk came in from Rexburg and Boise today. Been driving since three this morning, some of 'em."

"Okay?" says Pete Weiss in a low voice.

"Thing of it is," Dutch confides, "they decimated the ladies' room TP. Where can we get our hands on a couple more rolls right quick? Some of our people have serious toilet problems and we're gonna need a re-supply or there'll be some pretty unpleasant consequences."

"I don't know," says Pete Weiss, holding the phone away from the conversation like it might become contaminated. "I'm here from Billings."

Dutch sighs powerfully and dismisses Pete Weiss with the sheer force of his disappointment. Then he points at his sons and me and a few others, and leads us into the foyer, where he arranges us into search parties.

"We're looking for a supply room and-or a janitor's closet. Move out."

I stay behind. Larry gets the idea to roll some toilet paper from the men's room onto the empty tube from the ladies'. Guilt will do that, I guess—make you think something like that is a good idea. Or maybe he's done this before. In the corridor he sets up a two-man system with his half-asleep son, Taylor.

"Keep it straight," Larry scolds. "This will only work if it's straight."

"Larry," I say, "why not just put the whole roll in the women's bathroom?"

"Because we need some in the men's, too," he says with a worried look.

Taylor yawns.

Larry nudges me and says, "So, James, word is you

know why the big change in plans. Why we had to come clear out here instead of just burying him in Boise. It's about the Place, isn't it?"

I shrug again. Larry doesn't push it. He and Taylor roll the toilet paper.

Soon Dutch shows up with his searchers. He sees Larry and Taylor and says, "Oh, Larry, you are kidding me." He rubs his face, adjusts his tie to cover his collar gap.

"Leave us be, Dutch," says Larry.

"We found the closet, knucklehead, but it's locked." He marches into the chapel and does the horse whistle at full volume.

Everyone goes quiet for a moment. Heads turn.

In his booming, drill-sergeant diction, Dutch says, "Listen up, folks. Who here can pick a lock?"

Patricia stands at the chapel door and hisses, "Dutch, honey, you can't go around a church picking locks."

They discuss this.

Val comes over to the toilet paper transfer station. He furrows his brow at what he sees. Then he looks down at me for a few seconds like an owl on a phone pole.

"How you doing, kid?" he says.

"I'm okay, Val. You?"

"Good, good, real good. They're saying Dad told you why he wanted us to come way out here. What's the old guy up to, Jimmy?"

"He gave me a letter just before he went into the hospital. Told me to read it at the cemetery."

"Let's see it," says Val. He holds his hand out.

"I can't. He told me to read it at the cemetery."

"Jimmy, no. I need to see it. Hand it over." He holds his hand out.

Val's the oldest—Dad's second in command. Or he

was, back when me and my brothers were working around the Place, feeding the horses and chasing stray cows and hauling hay, we took as many orders from Val as we did from Dad. And Dad had warned me about him and my other brothers.

"They will try to override me when I'm gone, James," he'd said. "You gotta stand up to them. Tell them you're my executor. Say that to Val. Tell 'em I have a lawyer. They'll back down."

I look up at Val and repeat, "At the cemetery."

"He's messing with us, isn't he?" says Val. "Sneaky old bastard. Did he sell the Place? Who'd he sell it to? Crawfords? Just tell me. I won't say anything."

Larry stops rolling the toilet paper. "He sold the Place?"

"Course he sold it," says Val. "There wouldn't be a letter if he didn't sell."

"Jesus, James," says Larry. "Hand over that letter."

"At the cemetery," I repeat. I do my best impression of Dad's voice, or at least the baritone of it, the forcefulness of it. The bassy part that made us get moving again if he caught us lollygagging. I'm trying to project that part of Dad. I hope they don't notice. They'll gang up on me if they do. "These are his wishes, not mine."

Val grins bitterly, like he already knows what's going on and only needed to confirm it. He slips his hands into the pockets of his slacks, and he slouches. It's his way of backing down. He's twenty years older than me and a foot taller, but he's backing down just like Dad said. I can't believe it. It's like Dad's standing behind me in his overalls and workboots.

When I was a little kid, three or four years old, Val went into the Air Force. Then Bill went to Texas A&M,

and Dutch went into the Marines. Dad cursed them—in their bedrooms while they packed, in the driveway as they loaded their trucks.

"I need you on the Place," he demanded. "What am I supposed to do out here with no help?"

When the older brothers were gone, Dad broke down and got a hired hand, and that's when Ricky and Larry quit showing up for chores. Dad kicked them, threw feed buckets at them, but after a while, they moved away, too. Larry moved into Boise and Ricky bought a motorcycle and drove it all the way to New Mexico to get away.

That's when Dad started threatening to sell the Place out from under us.

"You don't know what you got here," he'd yelled at them on the phone. "This is land, the only real thing there is. I'll sell it all before I give it to you deadbeats. Sell it and buy two hundred acres of bare ground somewhere. Make you start over."

They didn't believe him back then, or they didn't care. Now, as we sit there in the chapel, I catch them looking at me. Now they believe.

Pete Weiss finally hangs up his phone and rounds us up in the chapel. He can't work the microphone, so he tries talking over everyone. I hear about every other word. What time things start, who's supposed to be where.

I touch the front of my jacket and think about Dad's letter, how I'll read it. I don't want to rush it. I don't want to blow it.

Pete Weiss tells the pallbearers to stand up, so we do.

Before Dad died, it never occurred to me that he had exactly the right number of kids to bear him to the grave. Six sons to carry his casket, two daughters to stay with his widow. Like he'd planned it that way. No one would put it past him.

There is just the one daughter now to comfort Mom—Deanne's gone, and I could swear that even now I see more tears for her than Dad.

Ruth pulls her duty like a goddamn yeoman, shepherding Mom from place to place, steadying her, toileting her. Perhaps most vexing of all is the task of addressing Mom's persistent stream of half-crazy babble, sorting her incoherent muttering from the questions that require actual answers. All of us brothers are desperately obliged that we don't have to deal with it. I promise myself to tell Ruth this before we all split up and go.

Pete Weiss takes the six brothers into the viewing room for a dry run. The casket sits on a gurney that we can roll into the chapel, but from there to the hearse we've got to horse it up some stairs and out across a pea-gravel parking lot where the gurney won't roll.

"The wheels'll just sink," says Pete Weiss.

Dutch says, "That figures."

Dad always joked about being buried in a pine box, so Val built him an old-timey coffin. It's pine, but dark-stained and lacquered and immaculately joined. The hinges and braces are from old barns and buckboards. The handles are made of horseshoes, fastened flat to the wood but bent outward to grasp. Val's been into woodworking since he was a kid. We've told him for years he ought to give up chasing government contracts and open up a cabinet shop. Dad's coffin is easily his finest work. He runs his hand along the coping. His eyes turn wet, though whether it's because we're burying Dad or the coffin itself, I'm not sure.

Pete Weiss positions us around the coffin according

to height and estimated lifting ability. Val and Bill are tallest, at the front. I'm across from Dutch, on the middle handles. Larry and Ricky are behind us.

"The key is to breathe," says Pete Weiss. "Breathe deeply and steadily. Don't hold your breath. Don't hurry. Guys in the front set the pace. Guys in the back, stay in step. So. Let's lift up your father so we can get an idea of the weight. Any questions?"

"Yeah," grumbles Dutch out of the side of his mouth, "what's this 'we' business?"

Dad weighed less than two-hundred pounds when he died. The coffin's at least another hundred and fifty. Seems like it should be about fifty pounds each, but it feels like more than that, a lot more. It's because of the horseshoe handles—they look rustic and exquisite and just as Dad would have them look, but they're not handles. They're horseshoes. They're slightly too small for us to get the good, baseball-bat grip we'd have on the handles of a factory-built casket. The angled sides of the coffin don't help, either. The edges of horseshoes cut into our fingers and squish our hands until our knuckles and fingers overlap. Everyone winces, even Dutch.

"These handles worked great when it was empty," grunts Val.

"Don't worry about it," says Bill. "It's beautiful. He'd be proud."

We all chime in to agree, but we set that coffin down right away.

After lunch, we take our places around the church for the viewing. Val stands by Dad. Pete Weiss posts a couple grandkids outside the doors as ushers. He puts Dutch in the foyer to direct traffic, as if Dutch wouldn't go out there and do that, anyway.

Then we wait, but no one comes. An hour goes by. Nobody. Everyone's looking at their phones. The grandkid-ushers abandon their stations. The other kids slip outside and play tag in the howling wind. They seem to be experiencing the best day in their entire lives.

We don't have deep roots in Montana. Mom and Dad are from there originally, but they moved out to the old family place in Idaho shortly after they got married, and Dad made it a going concern. We have relatives across the western states, but none of us are particularly connected even to Idaho. Val moved to Maryland while he was in the Air Force. Bill's lived in Texas for so long now he sounds like he's from there. Dutch moved all around in the service, landing back in Idaho almost by chance. Larry stayed around Boise but never worked the Place. No one except Bill ever saw much of Ricky at all.

The whole time, Dad kept on threatening until it became obvious no one was going to come back to work. After that it turned into a family joke. One year at Thanksgiving, Val and Dutch were really riding him about it.

"Two-hunnerd acres a' bare ground!" said Val, doing his impression of Dad, which is spot-on. Ten times better than mine.

We all laughed.

"Where was it gonna be, Dad?" chuckled Dutch. "North Dakota?"

"Siberia!" said Val. The two of them wheezed with laughter.

"Montana," growled Dad, slamming down a Corningware crock of yams. He was not laughing. "I know just where, too. Right along the Musselshell

River. You laugh, but I wasn't joking then and I'm not now. I'll leave you with nothing but bare earth, like when my Great Granddad started out."

"Doesn't make any sense, Dad," said Val, still half-kidding, still chuckling. "If you think we'll sell this place, why wouldn't we sell two hundred acres someplace else?"

"Oh Val, you're so damn smart," Dad snapped back, and the kidding was over. "You ever own any real property? I mean big tracts. Ever try buying or selling anything bigger'n a house on a half-acre? No. You haven't. It takes a toll on you. If you can't sell it, it needs to be making money, and when you do try to sell it, it sucks the life outta ya. Makes you so you can't trust anybody. It eats up your time—thinking about it, working on it. When you get an offer, you second guess if it's not enough, and it's never enough, and it sucks your life out. This is real. This is important. You want your birthright? Earn it. I swear to God I'll make you earn it."

Val and Dutch were quiet.

"If you sell the Place," said Dad, "there'll be a house on every single acre within ten years. Just little lawns and sprinklers and roads where you all hunted and camped and fished. You won't be laughing then."

We wheel Dad into the chapel for the funeral service. No one else comes. It's just us, but that's over a hundred people, and it's everyone—every one of Mom and Dad's kids, grandkids, and the few great-grandbabies. Everyone, right down to Ray. It's like a miracle. People are crying, laughing, hugging, taking pictures. We all get in line and walk past Dad in his pine box like a regular viewing line would.

"First time I've seen him since Dee's service," says

Ricky, "and here I got to wait in line to do it."

Next we settle back into the chapel and Dutch runs the show. Val gives the eulogy. Ruth plays her violin, Bill and Fran sing a couple songs. Considering it's a funeral, everyone's pretty happy, but word has gotten around about the letter.

Dutch takes the pulpit again and looks down at me. He looks at me for a few seconds, then says, "Anybody got anything to say before we head out? It's a good forty-five minutes to the cemetery."

Everyone cranes around to look at me. Val jerks his head at the pulpit. I don't answer.

"Fine," says Dutch, lifting his gaze from me at last. "Let's take the old guy for one last drive."

We line up around the casket and lift, grunting. The casket seems to be resisting us, shifting oddly, holding us back.

"You're not in step," whispers Pete Weiss. "Get in step."

"Left, right, left, right," Dutch chants in his drill-sergeant voice.

We finally synchronize, but my whole arm is throbbing before we're even outside. And the raked angles of the coffin make it so we don't line up straight, so we're kicking each other's feet as we go. Pete Weiss opens the side doors and wind whips into the chapel. If anything, it's blowing harder now. In the parking lot we catch grit in our eyes and teeth. We get Dad in the hearse and then stand in the wind, shaking out our clawed-up hands, and rubbing them. Our ties and jackets whip around furiously.

"It really is a handsome piece of woodworking," says Pete Weiss, "but I've had concerns about those handles since I first saw it."

Dutch looks like he's going to sock Pete Weiss in the mouth. "You shoulda said something," he growls.

"Yeah," says Val. "I could've swapped out those handles if I'd known last week."

"Well, I'm sorry," replies Pete Weiss. "But I called the caretaker. He's got a four-wheeler we can use to get the casket from the hearse to the plot."

Dutch scoffs. "My dad ain't going to his final resting place on some old four-wheeler." He flexes his hand. "It's not that bad. We'll carry him."

"No," laughs Pete Weiss, holding up a hand, "no, the plot is smack-dab in the middle of the section. It's a long way. Almost twice as far as this. And there's monuments to go around, and a tree."

"Ya shoulda said something earlier," says Dutch jabbing his finger at Pete Weiss.

"Easy," says Bill.

"I told you," says Pete Weiss, "we can use the four-wheeler. It's almost twice as far."

"We'll carry him."

It's more than twice as far.

We take Dad halfway, then set him down in the shade of a tree to rest our hands. Dutch's fat knuckles are bright red. The caretaker sits on his four-wheeler and slowly shakes his head. Wind rips around the cemetery, blowing hats and programs across the grass.

"Tell us what's in the letter," says Val before we start again. "Summarize. Hurry."

The others nod and grunt in agreement.

"No," I answer as I massage my hand. "I'm outta breath anyway."

The sun is coming low. Everyone's waiting at the plot, so we swap sides and pick Dad up again. We maneuver between the gravestones. It feels like a locomotive is parked on my hand and wrist.

"He sold it, didn't he?" grunts Val.

"When we get there," I mutter back.

"Did he or didn't he?"

"When we get there."

When Dad is at the excavation, we set him on the winch. Then our wives pat us on our backs and shoulders and help us to our seats.

I'm cradling my hand like it's an injured puppy, but it's time, so I stand up and pull the letter from inside my suit coat. Then I go to where the coffin sits on the winch, to the place where I stood with Dad and stared existentially at the ground just weeks before. My hands are so cramped and hot I have trouble unfolding the paper. It almost gets away from me. I've already read it two dozen times—I helped Dad write it, right here, sitting in this grass. Only now the letter looks different somehow, like a page from some ancient scripture.

Dad's instructions have the chairs facing east. I stand facing west, with Dad's grave between me and everyone else. They all look at me, their backs straight, eyes searching. I look down at the letter. I don't rush it.

"I never was going to sell the Place," I read.

Moans and gasps.

Val leans back in his chair, closes his eyes, and pinches the bridge of his nose. Bill beams a wry and placid smile, appreciating the grand scale of the jest, giving Dad his credit. Dutch wears a grudging smile, knowing he's been played, looking like he wants to sock me in the mouth.

Val was the first to say it out loud—that Dad went a little crazy after we all left. To support himself and Mom, Dad leased out big pieces of the Place, and he and Mom went to auctions and estate sales to keep themselves busy. Dad bought up antique saddles, tack, old farm equipment. He piled it up around the house. Then he ordered things off TV—gadgets, dietary supplements, so-called collector's items. He bought big bronze statues of horses and eagles and Indians.

A therapist friend of Cynthia's told us that older folks do that sometimes after they retire from exceedingly productive, work-oriented lives—they buy up things they don't need and hoard things they think are valuable. She said it's a way to maintain a feeling of security or control or stability.

Three years back, when we came home for Christmas, the house was so crowded with bronze statuary and exercise equipment we had trouble finding spots to sit down. Val suggested we ought to do something or say something about it.

"Go ahead and try," said Dutch, sitting in an easy chair with his feet up on some old exercise bike.

"Try what?" said Dad, coming into the room, winding through the trove.

Val gestured at the statues and tchotchkes and said, "Dad, you can't just—"

"Can't what?" said Dad. "Spend all my money? Why not? Still mine. Don't worry, I'll be out of your way faster'n ya think."

The wind rattles the letter in my hand like a kite. I read the next line loudly, kind of trying to do it in Dad's voice, or at least the way he would do it if he were me.

"But if I was to sell the Place and buy some bare ground to start over, this is where it would be."

I look up at them. Mom's eyes are clearer. Her hair is a mess in the wind, but she's looking at me with clear eyes.

"Now," I continue, still trying to get the voice right,

"get on your feet and take a look around."

They trade glances.

In my own voice tell them, "He wants you to stand up and turn around. Look that way." I point to the west.

They do it, one at a time. They're so relieved. Val puts his hands in his pants pockets and eases into his trademark slouch. Dutch does a precise, military-style about-face. We look out past the foot of the cemetery hill and to the valley below. The sun touches the mountains. The Musselshell River twinkles like a ribbon of tinsel.

"That is it," reads the letter. "That is the two-hundred acres out there. It's federal land now. It wasn't back then. They graze cows on it and there's some oil and gas development. But I like to think this is what our Place looked like a couple hundred years ago, before the fields, before the farm roads and fences. I'm sure you can see it. The way the hills kindly lean back on their haunches, the river coming down between."

The wind dies, suddenly. In later years, they'll say it was Dad's doing. No one would put it past him.

"It's gorgeous," intones Bill. "Sublime."

Then everyone is quiet. I'm not reading the letter anymore. Dad is.

"Nobody showed up, did they? Nobody but you all drove six hours to see an old crank planted. If we were in Boise you'd have the usual suspects. Faustina Nelson asking how you're doing every five minutes. She'd bring that rotten spaghetti casserole of hers. Not even the dog would eat it."

Everyone laughs nervously.

"Well, he's right about that," says Mom with a shrug and nod.

They laugh more.

"Olive Inverness would play 'Nearer My God To Thee' so slow you'd feel yourself getting nearer to Him whether you wanted it that way or not. Then Vic Olsen would show up in that infernal track suit of his to gloat that he's five years older'n me and still getting around, tell you how many miles he can jog. But he didn't come. And they didn't. It's just us."

Dad had a way of doing this, of predicting how something would go and then amazing everyone by being casually and frankly right about it. We all stand looking out over the countryside. Arms go to waists.

"I was wrong," says Dad. "There is only one thing that is real, but it's not land. Nor money, nor any dead or inanimate thing. I learned that much before I went. You all can go on home now. Watch over Mother for me. She's been cranky some mornings lately."

"Right again," says Mom.

We laugh.

"I'll hang back and watch over this valley. Me and James came here in April. While he was writing a check for the plot, I looked out over the valley and saw the ghosts of outlaws and Indians and bison passing by."

Mom leans into Ruth. Sobs rack her's little frame. Ruth holds her up. Bill and Dutch come to her side, then Val and Larry, and then even Ricky and Ray crowd in.

"I expect you all will sell the Place, and you'll cut up the land for backyards and parking lots. The money will go for college degrees and new cars. It's the way of things. I have made my peace by it. You can visit me here and look out and, in a way, you can at least remember where you come from, what you're made of: you come from the land, and you're made of hard work. Then again, you may want to start again. You may want to work the Place. If this is so, you're going to have to pipe those goddamn canals. Open canals are just too wasteful, too much maintenance. And the fences are gone to hell. And the footing of that second outbuilding by the well is subsiding at the northeast corner. Shore it up or the whole slab's going to crack. And there's other things. There's a list. But if this is so, if you work the Place, I'll rest even easier. And if you start over, say you started here."

AND ONCE SHE COULD FLY

Her name was Vira Anne. That was the first thing. Vira Anne was her name, she was eighty-eight years old, and she was originally from Musselshell, Montana.

When she awoke most mornings, these were the things she recalled. These things and one other: she once had the ability to fly.

How clearly she remembered stretching her arms out like some slender, tawny bird spreading its wings. She remembered the high, white clouds spread across the Montana sky and the ground far below and the air rushing over her bare skin, and through her hair.

Most mornings Vira Anne awoke before dawn, the window by the bed still dark. She lay watching it turn from black to indigo, and from indigo to the color of day.

With only her name and scarcely anything else to think about, her mind was like a room vacated and swept clean—uncluttered by furniture or flower pots or things unneeded. Peaceful, but not altogether comfortable.

Orderlies in pastel-colored scrubs brought her

breakfast and some hours later they brought her lunch. The difference between the two was not considerable— tiny plastic cups with foil tops and filled with cottage cheese or tapioca or applesauce. She ate in the bed, which had a motor underneath to hoist her into an almost-seated position. At some point the television was switched on, but Vira Anne could only listen to it because her eyesight had grown too poor to see the TV from across the room.

With voices from old TV programs and commercial jingles drifting through the air, Vira Anne remembered that she had lived in that care facility for ten years, though she could not name the place or the town it was in. Then she remembered that she'd lived in Sacramento before that. And back behind that, ancient Musselshell, Montana, and then at last the memory of flying.

Flight.

"But how could I fly?" she asked.

"How could you what?" answered a young man's voice.

"How could I fly? How could I have flown?" she repeated. "Do you know?"

"No," said the voice. "I don't."

It was another orderly. They were everywhere all the time. Sometimes they indulged the residents and sometimes they did not.

On most days Vira Anne would develop a clearer picture of herself by afternoon, around three o'clock, though actual facts were still in short supply. She had married and had children and had gone on to be a woman of some importance. She could remember that women and men alike had often deferred to her judgment.

Four o'clock is when they came for her.

"Hey, sweetie, it's Ruthie. Ready for dinner? Ready to get out and walk a bit? Let me fix your socks for ya."

This orderly had arrived entirely unbeckoned to pull Vira Anne stiffly from the bed and onto her feet. The care facility required that all residents walk a little each day if at all possible to maintain their strength and energy.

Vira Anne was stooped with her years, but she was taller than any of the other residents. She was taller than Ruthie and most of the other orderlies, too. They often had to team up to move her, call in an administrator or janitor for that little bit of needed extra muscle. Vira Anne had once stood a lean and formidable six-three. In those days she was tanned and freckled, and her thick red mane did as it pleased most of the time, even when she pulled it back with a stout rubber band. Now Vira Anne was pallid and spotted, and her hair grew thin and short, like a frizzy silver halo.

Not long after she arrived at the facility, Vira Anne calculated that it took her one full minute to walk twenty-five feet, though she had forgotten doing so and had slowed significantly since that reckoning. What she did now was not proper walking, anyway. She did not lift her feet or swing her arms. She could only squint at the floor and push her slippered feet forward a few inches at a time, never losing contact with the earth. With the TV switched off, the only sounds in the room were the polite encouragement of the orderly and the "shh-shh-shh" of the slipper soles on the smooth wooden floor.

"I used to could run," she announced. "I could run, and at one time I could fly."

The orderly murmured her approval and steered Vira

Anne wobbling to the door.

At five minutes after four or thereabouts, Vira Anne would clear the threshold of the room and shuffle out into the hallway where she would join other residents with other orderlies in the slow procession to the dining room. A parade of walkers and wheelchairs and shuffling old ghosts. When Vira Anne saw the hallway hung with drab acryllic still-lifes and watercolor landscapes, her mind would roll heavily back to the day she moved into the facility and with that recollection she would remember too that it was her children who sold her home and placed her here, they having grown too busy with their own children to care for her. At certain times, such as Christmas, they visited her.

She lived on the third floor of the facility and on the way to the dining room there was a breezeway that bridged two buildings. The walls were made of glass and as they crossed this breezeway Vira Anne looked blearily down at the nearby treetops and the roofs of the cars. Again the recollection of flight, of soaring.

She asked the orderly: "Do people fly these days?"

"Do people fly? Do you mean like in airplanes?"

"No," said Vira Anne. "Can people fly by themselves, in the air, when they're young, like you. Can you fly?"

"No, sweetie," she answered, "people can't fly unless they're in an airplane—or in a balloon, I guess. Helicopter. You know. Things that fly. Almost to your chair, sweetie. Doing good."

Even with the orderly's help, Vira Anne could not reach the dining room on foot. She didn't have the strength and so the orderly would place a wheelchair at the far end of her endurance. When they reached that limit, the orderly would swing the chair into position, lock the wheels, and bear Vira Anne backward into the vinyl seat.

The mob of shambling patients converged on the dining room. Smells of bread and gravy. The clank of silverware and plates. Soon Vira Anne was shoved up to a table where others sat eating. She saw their faces and through the blur of her failing eyesight they looked much like people she had known, and with them came a flood of names. Names of neighbors, names of friends. Elizabeth Chilton. Mel and Mindy McNeil. The names of her children came to mind, as if reporting for some curfew. Bud, Calvin, and Ronnette. A four-bedroom rambler in the suburbs. Her husband Loren and his aftershave. The blue and gold uniform he wore.

"I'm going to start working again," Vira Anne told Loren at breakfast one day long ago. "When Ronnette moves the rest of her things out, I'm going to make her room into an office."

Loren looked up from the papers and smiled and nodded. "I can build you some shelves along that one wall," he said. Then he put on his cap and rose to leave. He kissed Vira Anne on the head and on his way to the door said, "See you at the airport on Wednesday, right?"

Airport. Of course. Vira Anne looked from face to face around the table as the dining room murmured and clanked around them. They sat mouthing the soft, mild food.

"I could fly once," she announced. "I believe I may have been a pilot."

"Lawyer," answered a white-haired lady through a mouthful of mashed potatoes. "You were a lawyer, Vira honey. In Sacramento."

Vira Anne paused, her rheumy eyes blinking and cast down. She had been a water rights lawyer. Yes.

Settlement contracts with the Bureau of Reclamation arising from the Central Valley Project on the Sacramento River and its tributaries. Water allocations and disputes over irrigation. Water expressed in acre-feet. She'd been an authority on the river and its uses. She wrote a book about it. She became very well known. But these things did not require the ability to fly. She looked up.

"Yes," she said. "That's right. But I flew. I could fly, I'm sure of it."

A man sitting next to her shook his head. He pushed up his thick spectacles and poked the table with his finger. "Loren was the pilot," he said, voice dry and wispy. "Loren flew, not you. He flew for PanAm for twenty-some years."

Vira Anne lowered her eyes again, as though his answer was accurate but incomplete, accurate but not helpful. The others slumped at their plates and chewed slowly. After dinner, as Vira Anne glided along in the wheelchair on the way back to the room, she recalled a site visit to a concrete headgate on the Sacramento. She led a team of lawyers with their slacks tucked into choreboots trodding through a freshly plowed field to inspect the operation of a recently installed irrigation system.

Someone twisted a wheel to open the gate and the concrete box began to fill with muddy water. Whole families of mice that had been denning all winter in the as-yet unused inlet were ejected into the swirling flow. Within a few seconds, several dozen of them were spinning tail first in the cloudy vortex, sodden and miserable. When the headgate was full, the water began to drain from an outflow and the mice were sucked out one by one and sometimes in pairs. Soon there was only one, paddling hopelessly. But as the water rose, the tiny creature somehow caught hold of the rough concrete side and held itself there. Then it climbed inch by inch until it reached the edge of the box, where it leaped into the grass and was gone.

Soon Vira Anne slid back further until her memories most remote became more real and vivid than the present time and place. By the time the orderly rolled her back into the bedroom, Vira Anne was senseless, mouth agape, eyes staring. She sagged to one side and jostled lightly as the orderly locked the wheels of the chair.

She was a restless girl in Musselshell. Tall and freckled with her mane of wild red hair. She wore trousers and drove around in a Chevy pickup with a double clutch. Her dad and brothers taught her to hunt and fish, and at every occasion they considered her as ready and able as themselves.

"Do not cross her," Vira Anne's brother Craig said to Loren when they were young men. "And it's not because me and the boys'd come after you. It's her. That one is not afraid'a nothing. Not you, not me, not anything. I'm telling you for your own good."

On summer afternoons when she was just a teenager, Vira Anne might steal away from her chores, wearing cutoff jeans and a too-small tanktop. In the summer heat with the insects buzzing, she sat in a tree by the state highway to watch the cars and trucks rumble past showing out-of-state license plates, trying to figure out what those places were like by the look of the cars and the sound of the names of the states. New Mexico, Oregon, Alberta, Michigan. She spoke each aloud.

When the cars and license plates ceased to entertain her, she jumped down from her branch, took off her shoes, and balanced on the train tracks that ran alongside the highway. She skipped lightly down the sun-heated rail like some lithe country acrobat as the insects droned.

In the bedroom, the orderly had enlisted two others of her kind to help lift Vira Anne from the chair, and with a sort of clinical reverence they heaved her onto the bed.

"Ruthie, you working this weekend?" said one of them.

"Yeah."

"Me, too. What's wrong?"

"She's going," said Ruthie.

"Mm hm."

"She's on her way."

"Tonight?"

"Could be."

Soon Vira Anne came to a deep and rocky gorge where the tracks crossed over the Musselshell River on a high trestle bridge. It was her custom to walk out onto the bridge—despite having once had a close call with a freight train. She walked out onto the bridge, still balancing on the rail in her bare feet. When she reached the center of the bridge, she climbed out onto a buttress and gazed down into the gorge where the Musselshell glimmered far below like a trickle of mercury. A great current of air billowed steadily up like the earth's own exhaust, fluttering her tanktop.

She leaned out over the yawning space, extending one leg behind her as a counterweight, like a dancer. Then she readied her arms like wings. The air moved over her skin, lofted her hair, cooled her brow.

"Can I fly now?" she asked.

"Of course you can, sweetie," said a voice.

Vira Anne floated into the empty air and out over the gorge. Beneath her, she saw the forms of lesser birds on the wing. The entire countryside was aglow with the lowering sun. On the upwafting thermals she soared, circling endlessly.

Other books by Chadd VanZanten

CREEP FACTOR
www.amazon.com/dp/B07J3X1CM5

It's the feeling that something isn't quite right. The glance of a stranger that lingers too long. A coworker who appears out of nowhere. Creep Factor is thirteen deeply creepy short horror stories that explore the awkward, unnerving, and the terrifying. From backstabbing roommates to vicious pets, from murderous spirits to soul-wracking nightmares, Creep Factor covers the savagely weird to the merely ghastly.

ON FLY-FISHING
THE WIND RIVER RANGE
www.amazon.com/dp/1467140430

With remote waterways and unpressured trout, Wyoming's Wind River Range is the backcountry fly angler's mecca. In the alpine lakes and streams, trout may approach a dry fly two or more at a time, and an angler can cast for days without seeing another person, let alone another angler. But more than just a place to catch lots of fish, the range is also a place to disconnect from noise and networks and reconnect with oneself. In  a series of essays on misfortunate father-and-son backpacking trips, disaffected Boy Scouts, psychotropic deep-woods epiphanies and many other topics, author Chadd VanZanten offers not only a survey of the fishing and history of the Wind Rivers but a tour of personal landscapes as well.

ON FLY-FISHING THE NORTHERN ROCKIES

www.amazon.com/dp/146711801X

Anyone would be hard-pressed to find a pastime more emblematic of the western spirit than fly-fishing. Liberating, poetic, wild, soothing and inspiring, it pushes the boundaries of the mind. In essays ranging from introspective to ironic, angler authors Chadd VanZanten and Russ Beck distill the purest truths of fly-fishing into essential, often humorous rules of thumb. With kernels like "always tell the truth sometimes" and "all the fish

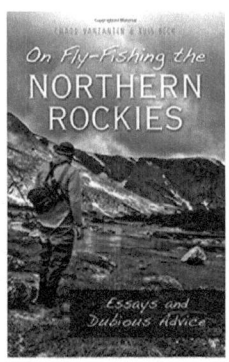

are underwater," wade into the blue ribbon waters of Montana, Idaho, Wyoming and Utah to reflect metaphysically on these lines of practical wisdom.

About the Author

Chadd VanZanten's short stories have appeared in numerous anthologies and collections, including *Creep Factor* (Knowledge Forest Press), *It Came from the Great Salt Lake* (Griffin Publishers), *Volatile When Mixed* (LUW Press), and *The Helicon West Anthology* (Helicon West Press). His outdoor essays can be found in his latest book, *On Fly-Fishing the Wind River Range* (The History Press), and in the fly-fishing magazine, *Fly Culture*. Chadd loves backpacking and fly-fishing, but is always eager to get home for the latest TV binge with his best friend, writing partner, wife, and muse, Amanda.

Follow him on Facebook:
www.facebook.com/onflyfishing